The Consolation Bride

UNEXPECTEDLY MARRIED
BOOK ONE

SARAH ZOLTON ARTHUR

Chapter One

"And so it begins." I leaned over to whisper to Gabby, my sister's best friend, as my mother, Mrs. Evelyn von Dutton—yes, of the Grosse Pointe Shores Von Duttons—clinked her crystal champagne flute three times to get everyone's attention. Her delicate, bird-like physique was accentuated by the golden cream silk dress that she wore tonight to upstage the bride in her stunning green. My mother and her magical superpower, her ability not to age. Flawless porcelain skin kept tight and elastic. Thick hair pulled up in a twist. We got the "are you three sisters?" question all the time.

It was a well-known secret that mother took trips to "rejuvenating spas" every couple of months and came back having shaved years off her appearance. Funny how the spa was located next to one of the country's most renowned plastic surgeons. She used to be a deep brunette just like my sister and me, but after each of those refresher visits, she returned with hair a little bit blonder than before. Evelyn considered aging a congenital disease that we Von Dutton women inherited from her and were expected to fight to the very end.

My father stood to her left and slightly behind her with his hands resting on her hips in his stance of solidarity. He looked as handsome as ever in his silk Armani suit. He felt no need to cover the slight graying at his temples because for a man, especially a man of wealth and power such as my father, gray looked distinguished.

"Thank you all for joining us today to celebrate the engagement of our beautiful daughter Gretchen and her perfect match, Mr. Stanton McCain. Gretchen and Stanton have been in love for as long as any of us can remember. We are so pleased to finally be uniting our families." My mother had a way of making every word out of her mouth sound pretentious. Like Mrs. Howell from *Gilligan's Island*. I held an affinity for vintage things such as vintage television shows thanks to my defacto-grandparents Alessandra and Rochester our married housekeeper and grounds chief who'd taken me and my sister under their wings years ago— without my parents' knowledge—and given us, or at least me, a relatively normal childhood when our parents were simply too busy to parent.

Everyone clapped. Of course they did. My eyes slid over to where the happy couple stood, Stanton's arm wrapped around my sister's waist, both of them wearing huge smiles. Beautiful Stanton, tall and broad-shouldered, with a face like a movie star. He wore his deep chestnut hair styled business cut but his most defining feature had to be his storm-cloud gray eyes. I sighed, momentarily forgetting myself. My sister in her emerald green silk looked just like our mother, but still wearing her naturally deep brunette hair twisted up in a ridiculously expensive updo. I tended to do my own hair. It was fun for me to play with styles and I'd gotten good at it over the years. Only a professional could touch my sister's locks. But maybe that was why *she* got Stanton.

Our fathers had done business together for years. Our mothers sat on boards for charities together and lunched regularly.

Stanton and Gretchen: the perfect couple. *Not.*

It wasn't sour grapes. I was happy for them if this was what they wanted, but I'd just never understood it. Ant and I—Ant, the name I'd called Stanton since probably the first day we'd been introduced as kids. "Stanton" had seemed too stuffy. Ant, he and I always had more in common. He loved going down to Comerica Park to watch the Tigers play. I loved going to Comerica Park to watch the Tigers play. Gretchen only went to PGA tournaments and tennis matches. Ant and I both loved the travel channel and cooking. Two things that my sister would have nothing to do with. Forget about eating a drippy burger, Gretchen never ate anything without a knife and fork unless it was an hors d'oeuvre like caviar.

Seriously, only two years separated my sister and me. So it wasn't like he'd be robbing the cradle. But for Ant, it had always been Gretchen. Maybe because of that more refined, highbrow nature or maybe because her boobs were about a half a cup larger than mine. It could've been her chiseled cheekbones or her deep, ocean-blue eyes. My cheeks had a bit more roundness to the apples and my eyes... Somehow, I'd ended up with a muddy brown.

The worst part for me had to be that my sister simply wasn't nice. The world revolved around Gretchen. If by chance, you found yourself in the position where you outshined her in some capacity, big or small, her congratulations came in the form of an obvious backhanded compliment.

Matthews, our butler, because yes, our family had a butler, approached my mother. "Ms. Von Dutton, lunch is ready to be served." He came to work for the family a couple of years ago after our first butler, Randall, retired. He was nice but kept to himself or the other staff, never engaging much in conversation with me. Tonight he wore his navy blue jacket with the family crest embroidered over the breast pocket. Again, *yes*, the family had a crest. My mother had the staff dress in uniforms at all times while out among the family and guests. Why? Just–why? But he learned the hard way, from what I'd been told after the fact because I'd still been away at school, that he learned the hard way to always defer to my mother in the presence of large groups. Parties were her artistic medium. Gretchen was the apple that didn't fall far from the tree.

"If everyone would please make their way to the dining room. Lunch will be served," Mother said.

Let me just say, the Von Duttons didn't do anything on a budget. There were so many options from seared swordfish to grilled eggplant, two kinds of pasta, one Italian white truffle, and one with lemon and walnuts. Soup courses. Salad courses and more dessert options than a small island nation could consume in a year.

Gabby, Gretchen's best friend, dropped into the seat next to me. She looked beautiful in black. She came from a well-respected Mexican-American family out of Texas. They didn't come close to the wealth and prestige of the McCains or Von Duttons, but they had enough means to allow her to continue to be friends with my sister. "Have you tried the swordfish?" she asked. "It's heavenly."

I shrugged. "It's not my thing." My mother had us eating off personally monogrammed china she'd purchased specifically for this lunch—white porcelain with real gold edging and letters. Talk about OTT. "But I can't wait to see how they top this at the wedding."

At least we didn't have to deal with a bridezilla. My family had the wealth to buy anything and everything Gretchen's heart desired. With that kind of cake tossed around, people didn't tell her *no*.

As we ate, more glasses clanked and the speeches started. Gabby's face fell and *she* sighed.

"What's wrong?" I asked.

"Oh, nothing."

"It's not *nothing*, Gabs. You don't sigh like that unless something's bothering you."

"Once she's married, she won't have much time for me. Your

mother already has her life planned out. The charities she's to join. All the dinner parties she's to host."

"You're her best friend. She'll always make time for you."

"No. Your mother has already set up play dates with your sister and other married socialites."

I popped out a laugh loud enough to catch the eye of Ant. I shrunk down in my seat and mouthed, "Sorry." But come on, *play dates*?

"What? I'm serious. She had lunch with Christina Rivers the other day. I've known Christina Rivers as long as Gretch has, but I wasn't invited."

"That doesn't mean—"

"Sylvie Sheridan was."

"My sister can't stand Sylvie Sheridan." Secretly, I couldn't stand Sylvie Sheridan either. If there was ever anyone on the planet to out-pretentious my sister, Sylvie Sheridan took that trophy.

"*Exactly*," she practically shouted with exasperation. "The only things those women have in common are wealth and husbands. I have a little wealth, but not a husband and that makes me a lesser class."

"Well, it's not much of a consolation, but you still have me."

She squeezed my arm. "The sister I never had."

Here's the thing. I really hoped Gabby was wrong about my mother, but as the lunch wore on, it became blatantly obvious that only the married couples got my sister's and Ant's attention for more than a few exchanges of "Thank you for coming" before my mother swooped in, shuffling them off to another table. Crappy, right?

Well, as it turned out, what they lacked in manners, my parents totally made up for with copious amounts of Dom Pérignon, of which both Gabby and I indulged until, for my part, I couldn't feel my feet and walking seemed more of a concept than a tangible state of being.

Gabby leaned in conspiratorially. "She's making a big—*huge* mistake." Either her words slurred or my hearing slurred. Fingers crossed on her slurring because I never met anyone drunk enough to have slurred hearing. "She doesn't want to marry him. He's a good guy, but they have nothing in common."

"That's what I'm saying," I slurred back, slapping the table hard, then I hiccupped because *hello*—classy. "You know she'll never make him happy the way he deserves." And I punctuated my point by waggling my finger in the air because nothing says '*I'm right*' like a finger waggle.

Ant looked so beautiful as he and my sister moved from table to table talking with their guests. In my opinion, nobody in the history of the world came close to everything that was Ant. As I scanned the room, I noticed a room full of tawny-haired men, but none of them had the richness of tobacco with the highlights and lowlights that I'd give almost anything to run my fingers through. The tiny flips and waves that never seemed to be tamable enough for my sister's taste. He caught my eye again for the briefest second. Every time he looked at me, it felt like looking into a thunderstorm.

Ah, well... Look at me waxing poetic.

It took them long enough, but they finally made their way over to Gabby and me gliding into the two empty chairs at our table to take a necessary reprieve from being the perfect couple entertaining their guests. Why did every thought in my head make me feel like a terrible person? I should be happy for Ant, finally getting what he'd always wanted.

"What are you doing?" my sister snapped at me low so only those of us at the table could hear.

I looked at her, dumbfounded. "Celebrating your engagement? Just like everybody else."

"Everybody else doesn't look a second and a half away from falling off their chair."

"Oh, no... I'd need to be *way* more drunk to fall off a chair."

Ant snickered and my sister shot him a "don't encourage her" glare that he completely ignored because we'd always been friends and I'd been making him laugh most of his life. Strangely, Gabby just sat there silently glaring at both Ant and my sister. She was really upset by this marriage. I understood. The four of us hung out all the time. The three of us—me, my sister, and Ant—growing up. Gretch met Gabby in college. Ant and Gretch applied and got into the same college, Brown University, the one I'd applied and gotten into two years later. Sure, my other friends or Ant's other friends would join us, but at the core were the four of us. Not that I particularly liked hanging with my sister all the time, but given the incomes of my friends in high school, my parents didn't trust my friendship decision-making skills. And now? We'd hit the end of an era. I doubted it would be too long before my sister pushed out those anticipated 2.5 kids, widening the gulch between us. That angered me even more. I wasn't ready to lose Ant to his responsibilities. I needed more time. *Gabby* needed more time–see? I wasn't being selfish. Altruism at its finest.

I cleared my throat and with a newfound sense of drunken stupidity or clarity, the jury was still out on which, I said, "I don't think you should do it."

"Do what?" Ant asked.

"Get married, *duh*. You're twenty-five. Why rush?"

"This is where it was always leading," he answered paradoxically. Why paradoxically? Because his lips tipped up in the corners indulgently as if speaking to a kid sister, but his eyes–if I had to give the look in his eyes a label, I'd call it resigned. "So why not now?" he finished.

Because I'm not ready, I wanted to scream yet I held my tongue saying nothing. Go restraint!

By his reaction, I didn't appear to have ticked him off, even though I internally kicked myself for blurting that out. My sister, however... Her face darkened to this beet shade of anger.

"Pen," she hissed, "just go." But Gabby placed her hand on my sister's arm, causing Gretchen to close her eyes and compose herself. "You don't have to go, but for God's sake, sober up."

She stood up to leave. Ant stayed seated a moment longer before joining her. "I'm done," I said to Gabby, pushing up from my chair. I'd be lying if I denied that my gaze lingered on Ant as he and my sister laughed at something some other guest had said.

Today totally sucked.

Chapter Two

My eyes aggressively popped open to the feeling of someone shaking me. It took a couple of seconds for them to adjust to being awakened and focus on the fact that a.) it was still dark out, b.) I had a screaming hangover, and c.) my sister was the one shaking me instead of snuggling up with her intended after a night of off-the-charts canoodling to celebrate their love.

Of course, I had no idea if Ant's skills in the bedroom matched my imagination, but my intuition said *yes*, and my intuition rarely failed me.

"Is there a reason you're waking *me* at the buttcrack of dawn instead of your fiancé for some morning nookie at his place?"

"*Yes*," she hissed, rolling *her* eyes.

"Well? Some of us need our beauty sleep."

"Sleep? Really? This is my life, Pen."

"And you own the patent? Because I'm pretty sure *this*"—I pointed to myself—"is *my* life. So again, I ask: Is there a reason you're waking me at the buttcrack of dawn?"

"I was up all night thinking about what you said."

Now that my eyes focused enough to get a good look at her, she definitely sported some pretty nasty circles around her normally gleaming eyes. Circles *Evelyn von Dutton* would be none too pleased to see on the bride-to-be, leading me to believe that she told the truth. Neither my sister nor I were prone to drama. We weren't allowed. Von Duttons didn't do drama and that scared the bejeezus out of me. Not that we didn't do drama, but that I'd said something bad enough to make my sister rethink marrying the only man she'd ever loved.

"What exactly did I say?" My stomach twisted, starting to go rancid, and I had a really bad feeling that I might have let that big ol' feral cat out of the bag. If I told her I was in love with Ant—

"You said that we were rushing into this," she replied, cutting off my downward train of thought. "You said we were both only twenty-five, so why go through with it now?"

"And you thought it was okay to give even a moment of headspace to anything that came out of drunk me's mouth?"

"Pen, please be serious. I'm trying to tell you that I don't think I can go through with this."

Oh, crap.

"Why are you telling *me* this?" She and I were sis-frenemies. Sister frenemies. I didn't trust it.

"You're so good at you know"—She flipped her hand in the air—"expressing emotions. I need you to tell Stanton."

My mouth dropped open. What in the holy no way?! It was probably not a secret to anyone but my family, Ant's family, Gretchen, or Ant himself that I really didn't want them to go through with it. She'd crush him if she didn't, though. He'd been in love with her forever. If she didn't marry him, what would that do to him?

Well, this wasn't how I pictured the morning after my sister's engagement party going, but somebody had to be the rational adult around here, and apparently, today that fell on me. God help us all.

I pushed up from under the covers to sit next to my sister, turning to her, and squared my shoulders. I pulled up my calmest authoritative voice and everything. And make no mistake, it gutted me to say this, but for Ant, I sucked it up.

"Listen, Gretch," I said. "You and Ant have always known you were going to get married. You love him. He loves you."

"It's not as easy as that," she replied. "I don't love Ant in a way that a woman should when she's going to get married."

"Gretchen, would you listen to yourself? You have *years* of togetherness under your belt. If you didn't love him, you'd have said so ages ago. The invitations have already been ordered. The halls have already had deposits put down. The—"

She cut me off. "That's another thing—who has more than one hall for a wedding? The hall for the bridal shower, the hall for the reception, the hall for the after-reception, the hall for God-knows-what-else. I feel like Mother's show pony." Well, this came as news. I always considered Gretchen "Little Evelyn." She reveled in the attention poured on her by being the eldest Von Dutton daughter. The one to bring pride to our family by joining us with the McCains. "I think Mother has already started planning my baby shower and I'm not pregnant," she continued. "I'm not planning on getting pregnant, at least not for a couple of years."

"There are positives and there are drawbacks to every family dynamic. We've grown up with a lot of privilege, you can't deny that. The flip side of that is you have to put up with Mother booking multiple halls for your wedding."

"Easy for you to say. You're not the firstborn. There are no expectations on you for merging the families."

I sucked in a sharp breath as if she'd punched me. No, it was true I might not have been responsible for merging the families, but that didn't mean I got to live this carefree existence. She wasn't around to hear Mother constantly harassing me about why I hadn't met a nice, young gentleman yet. The sole purpose of my attending Brown was to refine my education enough to land me a proper husband—because Von Dutton women didn't work. We supported our husbands in any way that would help advance *their* careers. What would the women at the club think if I couldn't land myself a man? Oh, the humiliation! The name Von Dutton ruined forever!

The words always stayed perched on the tip of my tongue, that I met a nice, young gentleman forever ago, but that he was in love with someone else. Much to my chagrin. But it wouldn't have done any good. Expressing my feelings for Ant meant opening myself up to being chastised by the entire family. That was something I could do without.

"Listen," I said. "This is just cold feet. You know when you dig deep and think about it that marrying Stanton is the right thing to do. He'll give you a beautiful life."

She sat there for a while staring down at her hands folded in her lap. She sighed and said, "You're right. I was just being silly. Stanton will give me a beautiful life. You may go back to sleep now, Pen." Then she pushed up off the bed but turned back to me for a second. "Best not to tell anyone about this." Then she left my room. Crisis averted, I rolled back over and forced myself back to sleep. It wasn't easy, as I had to fight off my own heartbreak to do it, but I did it.

Go me.

Chapter Three

My phone rang waking me up from a dead sleep and I flung my hand out, groping my side table trying to find the damn thing. This was my life since graduating five months ago. Sleeping in because I had a hard time falling asleep after staying up way too late lamenting my mother's progressively forceful determination to marry me off. How one might ask, did she accomplish this? Why, by setting me up on dates with men that I could never in a million years picture myself seeing even one more time. Pretentious. Up their own asses. Last night's winner worked at his family's bank. Yes, *bank*. And most banks were conglomerations now. His family had money. A fact he let everyone know practically everywhere we went, which happened to be dinner at one of the most expensive restaurants in Detroit and the symphony.

The way he treated our poor server when she accidentally splashed some water onto the table because *he* wasn't paying attention and threw his arm out, hitting her—the things he said. I was humiliated by his behavior.

"Robert, please stop," I said. "It was an accident."

He glared at me through his beady rat eyes. He looked handsome enough in his Alexander Amosu suit—because simple Armani wouldn't be enough to show his level of wealth to the masses—his blonde hair cut and styled perfectly. But the longer I sat with him the uglier he grew.

"You would think, *Penelope,* that an establishment with the reputation of La Belle Vie would hire proper employees rather than stoop to sending us an ignoramus who isn't fit to lick the dirt from my shoe."

The poor girl gasped and rushed away.

"Robert. That's enough." Because of my parents' connection to his family, I couldn't embarrass the good name of Von Dutton, thus, my water glass stayed full and not dumped over his head, but I excused myself to the restroom. My intention was to seek out our server, who I found crying in the kitchen. I hugged her, apologized profusely, and let her know that we'd been set up on a date and that I in no way approved of his behavior.

Yeah, so that was my night.

Now, my eyes barely registered as slits. Finally, my fingers grasped hold of the receiver, and I brought it up to my face to check the time. Seven a.m. Why on Earth was—I looked at the name flashing across the screen—my mother? Why on Earth was my mother calling me at this time of the morning?

I pressed the *answer* button. "Hello?" I said in a groggy voice.

"Penelope, we have a problem."

What kind of problem would *we* have? My parents hired people to take care of problems, which meant this call probably had to do with some bridesmaid backing out of the bridal shower today. Let's file that under *not* my problem. Anything else could wait until Monday.

Several months already passed since the engagement party —*wow*, I found that hard to believe. Wedding preparations were in full swing. They had been for a while now. I'd gotten a little nervous the day after the engagement party, that morning when my sister woke me up, but after we talked it out, she was good with things. I let out a slow breath. "What kind of problem?"

"It's your sister," my mother said. She sounded as if we were facing a life-or-death situation, which woke me right up.

I sat up in my bed, rubbing my eyes. "What about Gretchen?" I asked hurriedly. "Is she okay?" We might have had our differences, but that didn't mean I wanted something bad to happen to her.

"That's just it, I don't know. I can't get a hold of her. We have all the final checks to go over for the bridal shower today and every time I call, she doesn't answer."

"It's early. Maybe she's having a little fun with Stanton. You've checked her room?"

"Of course we've checked her room. I sent Nadine to wake her up an hour ago." An hour ago? What in the world would need to be done at six o'clock in the morning? And poor Nadine. She was one of our housekeeping staff. My parents paid her well, but did any job pay well enough to have to be up and on the clock at six A.M. on a Sunday morning?

"Okay, so did you call Stanton to find out if she's over there yet? Fair warning, if she is, he might not answer, either."

"We decided not to bother Stanton if it weren't necessary. I'll call him now and check if she's there. But you need to call Gabby. She might know where Gretchen is."

"I'll call. And if I can't get a hold of her, I'll go over to her apartment."

"Good, good, good... But remember, the bridal shower starts at one and you need to be there. So make sure you've dressed appropriately," she said. Because I hadn't been going to these types of uppity functions my whole life. I pinched my eyes shut to check my attitude, not wanting to add to my mother's stress.

"Yes, Mother, I'm fully aware of how I'm supposed to dress. I'll call Gabby. If I can't get a hold of her, I'll shower and get dressed. I'm wearing the navy sleeveless just like you wanted. Then I'll head over to Gabby's apartment to check things out."

My mother hung up on me without saying goodbye. Why did she seem to be in such a tizzy? My sister knew today was her wedding shower. Not to mention, this was hardly the first time she'd gone off with Gabby, or Stanton, to spend the day together and not answered her phone. I figured when you thought the world revolved around you, then there wasn't anyone to answer to.

As promised, I scrolled through my contacts until hitting Gabby's number and pressed the button. Then I waited... and waited... and waited as the phone rang and then went to voicemail.

"This is Gabby. Thanks for calling. I can't answer my phone right now, so leave a message and I'll be happy to get back to you just as soon as I'm able. Have a great day."

I waited for the beep. "Gabby, have you seen my sister? Is she with you? She's not answering her phone and my mother is absolutely freaking out. If she's with you, have her call back. It's important."

Okay, no luck on the Gabby front. I pushed up out of bed and walked over to my bathroom to get my shower going. Once finished with that task, I blew out my hair, wrapping it in an elegant, bridal shower-worthy chignon. Bridal shower makeup came next—and yes, believe it or not, there was such a thing as bridal shower makeup, just ask my mother. Lastly, I slipped on my sleeveless, navy-blue dress. It had a respectable boat neck collar, an empire waist, and a fitted skirt that fell to just below my knees. I paired that with my sweet navy heels and a navy-blue, wide-cuffed shrug jacket that had a band of white going around the sleeve by each wrist.

Of course, I wore the pearls. An elegant pearl necklace gifted to me by my grandmother on my sixteenth birthday along with pearl studs.

Before I left for Gabby's apartment, I grabbed up my navy-blue clutch and my wide-brimmed navy-blue hat. The entire ensemble reminded me of something Audrey Hepburn would've worn. I felt very elegant but not stuffy.

Rochester had my SUV pulled out of the garage and waiting for me, engine running. He kept the keys hanging in the garage because heaven forbid we parked our own cars. But I digress.

"Thanks, Rochester," I said, smiling at him. Rochester was a wonderful man, even after all the years he spent working for us, which would have driven me nuts in his position. Evelyn wasn't cruel like Robert last night, but she definitely let *"the staff"* know their places in the hierarchy of our home. He turned his grandfatherly type, warm eyes that always smiled, on me. And although very professional around my parents, he gave words of kindness or advice to my sister and me even with a simple glance. I loved him and Alessandra. I still loved spending time in their spacious apartment above one of the garages cooking and playing card games. She started out as one of our housekeepers, but as that tended to be a rather physical job, she'd been promoted to manager. So now it was her job to delegate duties to the other housekeepers.

Given that I never knew my mother's parents because they passed away before I was born, and my dad's parents, well... My grandmother called me *pet*, and I wasn't allowed to call either of them "Grandma" or "Grandpa." No, by official decree, we were to only call them "Muffy" and "Skeeter."

Oh, yeah—*Muffy* and *Skeeter*. That pretty much summed up my childhood.

Anyway, given all that, Rochester and Alessandra took to us as little girls and loved us the way only grandparents could. When it snowed they made us cocoa and when we were hurt, they bandaged scraped knees. Despite my privileged upbringing, my childhood would've sucked without them.

"Where you off to so early on a Sunday?" he asked.

"Today is Gretchen's bridal shower and we can't get a hold of her."

A look of genuine grandparenting concern crossed his face. "Do you think she's okay?"

"Oh, I'm sure she's fine. This is not the first time my sister has gone off and not answered her phone. Remember that endowment benefit gala a couple of years back?" The whole family was supposed to attend. It was the event of the year organized by my mother, Mrs. McCain, and the other women on the endowment board. Ball gowns. Dignitaries. More money than even I could fathom exchanging hands for good PR and a hefty tax write-off. Gretchen didn't show up until ten minutes before seating ended. My mother and father were livid, but that was classic Gretchen.

"Well, if you need any help looking for her, you have my number."

I smiled at him again. "I sure do." Then, with a head nod telling him that I was ending our conversation, I slid into my SUV, shut the door, and clicked on my seatbelt. I drove a sporty, silver Mercedes Benz G-Class that my parents gifted me when I graduated from Brown earlier this year.

Don't get me wrong, I appreciated the car. But... two hundred grand seemed excessive. They could have spent half that or less and donated the rest to a charity of my choice in my name. But they didn't and I refused to look a gift horse in the mouth. I took off down the drive and turned out onto the street heading in the direction of Gabby's apartment located about an hour's drive from our home in a nice neighborhood—but you know, not *Von Dutton* nice.

Only about two miles before I reached her complex, my phone lit up with my sister's name. Thank goodness. I press the green button to answer.

"Gretch? Where are you? Mother's going crazy. You have to get to the hall for the bridal shower."

"I'm not going."

Oh my god, my sister was such a nut. I laughed into the receiver until I realized that she wasn't laughing with me, and moreover, she actually sounded serious.

"What do you mean, you're not going? Gretch, this isn't funny. You have your bridal shower today, you have to show up.

It's kind of in the description. The bride needs to be there for her *bridal shower*."

"Well…" She sucked in a breath. Why would she suck in a breath? At that moment, I felt it in my gut that she was about to hit me with something very, very bad. "I can't make it to the bridal shower because I'm in Vegas."

"*Vegas?*" I sort of screeched into her ear. "What the hell are you doing in Vegas? You would have had to have left—"

"Last night," she said, cutting me off.

"So?"

"So… I got married."

"You and Stanton flew to Vegas to get married?" I felt the twinges of a really bad migraine about to start. "After all of Mom's planning?"

"I—*um*—I'm not with Stanton."

Wait, wait, wait… I slammed on the brakes. Car tires screeched behind me, their owners honking angrily. Several people shouted obscenities out their windows. *Shoot*—my bad. In my defense, they couldn't know the crisis I faced inside my car at this very moment, but once I got my wits together, I moved off to the shoulder so as to not continue to block traffic. "What do you mean, you aren't with Stanton? If you're not with your *fiancé*, then who, pray tell, did you marry?" I never felt this level of lividity before in my life.

"Penelope… You have to understand. I'm not in love with Stanton. I've never been in love with Stanton. The only reason we started dating was because that was what they expected of us— Mom, Dad, and the McCains. 'Turning two powerful families into one indomitable force.'"

Oh, yeah, my stomach clenched and my head hurt so badly now. Good thing I didn't eat this morning so that when I puked, there wouldn't be anything to come up and mess my face or dress.

"And you couldn't have decided this when he proposed? What is this going to do to him? You're going to crush the best man we know."

"I know," she said sadly. "But I had to follow my heart."
"Gretch, who did you marry?"
"My best friend and the love of my life."
"Gretch... *Who* did you *marry*?" I asked again.
She sighed and then answered, "*Gabby.*"

Chapter Four

I *'m sorry?* I couldn't wrap my head around this. Did she — did she actually say *Gabby*?

"*Gabby?*" I screeched into the line. "*Gabby?*" I screeched a second time, even louder. Of all the scenarios I could've ever pictured in my head, I never pictured this. "Okay... Okay, it's gonna be all right," I mumbled to myself.

"Pen?" my sister said.

"*No*—no, Gretchen, you had your time to talk. Now it's time to let me figure out what the hell I'm going to do, what I'm going to tell Mother, how I'm going to help Stanton, what we're going to do with all these guests who are showing up today for *your* bridal shower."

My pulse throbbed behind my left eye, causing it to twitch significantly. I loved Gabby—loved her like a sister, and now I guess she *was* my sister in a way. My reaction to this news had nothing to do with Gabby, nor did it have anything to do with Gabby and Gretchen falling in love with each other. My reaction came solely from the fact that my sister had years to deal with this, to come clean, to tell our parents, and more importantly to tell *Ant* who she was and what she wanted from her life, and she never said one word. Ant didn't deserve this, and now I was going to have to be the one to pick up the pieces of his broken heart. I'd be lucky if he ever talked to me again, with his humiliation off the charts.

"Gretchen, I have to go. You need to call Stanton, and you need to call Mother. I'll make your excuses at the shower."

"I thought you could do it for me," my sister said, blowing my ever-loving mind. I could tell she really meant it, she wanted *me* to do *her* dirty work. "It would make things easier if you called Stanton, don't you think?"

"Easier for who, Gretch? We've never much liked each other, but I've always respected you. Now though, if you don't call Stanton and come clean, I will be so, so disappointed in you. To the point that I don't think I'll ever get over it."

At least half a minute of dead air hung between us before my sister sighed then said, "I don't know what you're being such a baby about, but fine, I'll come clean." And then she hung up.

I probably should have said *congratulations* just once, but the way she'd handled this was beyond anything I thought her capable of doing.

Giving myself another moment to collect my thoughts, I took in a long, slow breath and then let it out even slower, a tip my therapist taught me to calm my anxiety. Once I felt ready, I clicked on my blinker, checked my mirrors, and merged back onto the road.

My body and my mind stayed disconnected from my heart. My heart told me this wasn't my problem. Gretchen had gotten herself into it, she needed to dig herself out of it. Whereas my mind, oh—my mind was full of thoughts I never imagined I was capable of possessing. Most of them included murdering my sister and stuffing her body into a garbage bin for the rats to feast on—*no, Penelope. That's not nice she's your sister and prison orange isn't your color.*

My body didn't care at all whether my heart and my mind were at odds because it drove me straight to hell, or excuse me, I meant the *hall*. I did *not* want to get out of my car. Yet again, my body betrayed me. My hand opened the door, my foot stepped out, followed by my other foot, and the next thing I knew, my body was walking me to the front entrance, where my mother stood wringing her hands.

Crap.

"Did Gabby have any news?" my mother asked worriedly.

"Oh, she had news, all right."

My mother's body stiffened. "What do you mean by that?"

"Mother," I said in the calmest voice I could muster. "Please, walk with me in the garden."

"We don't have time for that. Guests are already starting to arrive."

That certainly wasn't the best news. Still, I pressed my hand to her back ushering her in the direction of the hall's beautiful garden full of blossoming flowers of all varieties. Pinks. Reds. Yellows. Tall, sculpted topiaries. A fountain. Ornately casted cement benches. My words would sting but the scenery might soften the blow. Best to just rip it off like a Band-Aid. "Gretchen called me."

My mother cut me off. "Great." Her relief was palpable as her shoulders slumped just slightly. "How far away is she?"

I started to laugh like a damn fool. I couldn't help myself. "Oh, about two thousand miles away."

My mother abruptly stopped walking. She turned her head as slowly as a possessed doll and she looked *just as pissed* as one. Pissed wasn't a word we were allowed to use. Too common. Too crass. But at this time, it was the only word I could think to express the way my mother looked right now, with her mottled, red face and eyes set as hard as granite. I didn't want to be the one to test this theory, but while looking at her, it occurred to me that she just might be mad enough to lift a truck or punch a hole through a brick wall.

"Why, Penelope, is your sister two thousand miles away instead of here for her bridal shower?" my mother asked tightly.

"Because she's in Vegas."

"Are you saying that your sister decided to ditch her own wedding shower because she had an urge to play the slots?"

"I have no idea if she's playing the slots. What I'm saying is that she ditched her own wedding shower so that she could get married."

Relief of a sort flashed over my mother's face. "So she and Stanton decided to elope? It's not ideal, but we can spin this. The pair who were so desperately in love, they couldn't wait another moment to become husband and wife."

Unfortunately, it was up to me now to crush that relief. "That would work if she'd married Stanton." A vein pulsed in my mother's neck to the point that I worried she was about to have an aneurysm, and I wondered if I should tell her the rest.

She took that choice away from me when she demanded, "Whom did she marry?"

"She married Gabby, Mother." There, I did it. I did my part. Strangely, my mother had nothing to say about this news.

Even more strange, as abruptly as her mood started, it stopped. She ran a hand over her hair to straighten it and then both hands down the front of her dress. She straightened her posture again, looked at me, and said, "Yes, then you will accompany me inside now so we can take care of this mess."

Arm in arm, I walked back to the hall with my mother. Then I held the door to allow her through first. What I expected was for my mother to call attention to the room and explain to all the ladies in attendance that the wedding had been called off. But that wasn't what happened.

Oh, no, no, no—what she did was so much more diabolical. She placed both of her hands on each of my shoulders and said, "My daughter and I thank you all for showing up today."

Mm-hmm, she honestly said that. Oh, but it got worse. She led me to the seat of honor and pressed down on my shoulders until I got the hint that I was supposed to sit.

Some of the guests looked very confused, as they'd known both Gretchen and me for years. And others who were the wives and daughters of my father's associates had no idea they were currently being played.

I went through the motions of the shower. Giving the speeches my sister was supposed to give, and opening the gifts my sister was supposed to be opening. Why? Because as a Von Dutton daughter, I wasn't allowed to cause a scene. Remember, no drama. I did what my mother told me to do because she was my mother. Period.

Yes, it sounded pathetic even to me.

Yes, I needed to gain a backbone and stand up for myself. Easier said than done. I relied on my parents financially, for a place to live, for pretty much everything. Aside from the two years when I was on my own in Providence after Ant and Gretchen graduated—although my parents still paid for my apartment and all of my living expenses, not to mention my college education—this life was the only one I'd ever known. The idea of suddenly finding myself penniless and homeless because I spoke up for myself scared the bejeezus out of me.

Poor Penelope, right? Me and my first-world problems.

The worst part, however, was having to smile when someone called, "Gretchen, dear, you look wonderful. Congratulations on your impending nuptials." or "Penelope? I thought it was Gretchen who was marrying Stanton." My mother smiled and pretended like she never heard them, seamlessly moving the focus to something or someone else in the room. This went on until every last guest had left the hall and the workers had loaded up all the gifts into a truck to be driven to the house that my sister and Ant were supposed to share.

My headache only got worse from there. You better believe I got the hell out of there as soon as earthly possible.

The drive home happened without my control, on rote memory, turn by turn. It was a good thing nobody was out because I didn't know that I wouldn't have run them over without a second glance.

Rochester met me at the house, where he helped me out, and

I dazedly made my way inside as he parked my SUV in the garage. I walked up to my room, locked the door, then proceeded to take the longest, hottest bubble bath imaginable.

Once finished, I pulled all the shades in my room, threw the curtains, pulled on a nightshirt, and fell into bed. I didn't have it in me to *people* one moment longer.

If only I could've stayed in that blissful slumber for the rest of my life but oh no, reality hit me by pounding on my door.

"Miss Penelope," Nadine shouted at me through the door. "You need to get up and get dressed. Your parents are awful upset right now."

"Go away," I answered groggily. "I've done my part."

"No, you haven't. Your parents have called a big family meeting. The McCains are on their way over right now, so you need to get dressed, but you need to look respectable."

Well, that piqued my interest. "All the McCains? Is Stanton coming, too?"

"*All* the McCains," she said, stressing the "all."

I'd been his friend for years. Ant needed me. Right. I pushed up out of bed and set to dressing respectably for our guests.

"There she is," Mrs. McCain said as she hugged me, then pressed a kiss to each of my cheeks. "Penelope, it's so lovely to see you here." Like Evelyn, her hair mysteriously changed a shade blonder every couple of months and she too looked young enough to be Ant's sister. Though, I honestly liked Mrs. McCain. She loved her children, doted on them. Sometimes I thought that if she'd joined another family, she might've been allowed to be the kind of mother she had it in her to be.

Rather than still donning the dress she wore to the shower today, Mrs. McCain sported a pair of tan slacks with a defined press down each leg, and a white short-sleeved button-down. Mrs. McCain had a beautiful figure that she passed genetics-wise to her daughter who currently went to school in Vienna, thus she'd been unable to make it to the shower or this very important family meeting.

So lovely to see me here? It wasn't like I had a choice. I'd been summoned. Still, I smiled as I walked with my mother and Mrs. McCain into the formal dining room, where I took a seat next to Ant.

"How are you holding up?" I whispered to him.

"I'm okay. She and I had a long talk earlier this afternoon. I wish she would've talked to me sooner, but it is what it is."

"Are you sure you're not about to go shoot up a post office or something?"

He whipped his head to look at me, his eyes laughing as much as they looked confused and a bit startled. Yes, I'd known Ant long enough to glean all of that from a look. He had very expressive eyes.

"What?" I asked. "You're taking this far better than the situation calls for. I'm afraid you'll snap."

"I'm fine, Pen. I won't be shooting up a post office anytime soon."

For encouragement, I gave his knee a squeeze under the table. He raised his eyebrow at me, then turned his attention back to my father when my father's phone rang.

My father swiped to answer, then pressed the button to put the call on speakerphone. "Gretchen, you called. That was the responsible thing to do."

"I owed Gerald and Helena that much," she said in a tone filled with what I thought was supposed to sound like remorse. Maybe. Possibly. "I owe Stanton so much more than that." Okay, just no—every word out of her mouth sounded disingenuous, almost as if she were reading from a script to appease the families.

"I'm glad we agree," my father said, then he looked to the rightfully stern-faced Gerald McCain who looked like an older version of Ant. Handsome, but with a bit of gray in his hair and lines on his face. He only wore dress, business or business casual clothing. And given his attire now, that being business casual, I figured he and my father had been pulled from the golf course to attend to this pressing matter. "Your mother and I have come to a decision. You've embarrassed us beyond measure. The McCains are our closest friends."

"I know," my sister replied, cutting him off.

"I wasn't finished. Gretchen, you will stop this nonsense. You will come home and you will marry Stanton or you will be cut off."

My sister gasped. Stanton shot his hand out in front of him. "No," he said quickly and looking more than rather astonished that my father had even suggested such a thing. "She's married. It's done."

"So what is your decision, Gretchen?" my father asked. "Do you plan to stay married to Gabby?"

"Yes," my sister said defiantly.

"Then we are done here," he replied. He pressed the button to end the call. Both Ant and I stood from our seats, ready to get the heck out of there until my father shook his head at us. "Done with *her*, not with *you*."

Gerald stood and walked around the table, stopping behind Helena, where he placed both hands on her shoulders. "The reason for this wedding hasn't changed. The Von Duttons and the McCains are two very powerful families separately. We would be an indomitable force together."

I narrowed my eyes at the man while trying to figure out exactly what he meant. He didn't make us wait long to find out.

"*Stanton*—Philip and I have talked it out and we've come to an agreement that will benefit everyone."

"And that is?" Stanton asked.

"Since Gretchen is now off the market, and has refused to make amends for her mistake, Penelope will take her place."

My head jerked back painfully as I choked on a sudden mouthful of saliva. Ant patted my back to make sure I didn't die while the parents tuned us out completely. I could have argued. I *should* have argued. But people were expecting Ant to marry a Von Dutton daughter. Nobody cared which one. And besides, it had been decided. I heard what they said to my sister. Cutting her off because she dared to disagree with them. I wasn't naïve enough to believe that I'd be fine without my parents' money. I'd been graduated from college, from Brown University, for several months and I still didn't have a job. They'd never meant for me to get a job after graduating unless you counted finding a suitable husband who would help add to the prestige of the Von Dutton name. Have this man's children. Only two. And support him in every way that was him until the day I died. The funny thing—from the moment I discovered boys *that way*, it'd only been Ant. Years of longing to be where I was right now. Only now, I wasn't the grand prize. I was the consolation—the participation trophy and that hurt.

Stand from the table, Pen. Tell them no—that your life is your own. Then walk away.

Stand from the table? Walk away? Laughable. No, I knew the moment the words came out of Gerald McCain's mouth that I'd go through with it.

It was just... It was one thing to play Gretchen for a day. It was another to now have to live her life.

Chapter Five

Ant grabbed my hand, pulling me up from the table. He led me out of the dining room to where we could speak privately. Dropping my hand, he turned me to face him.

"What do you want to do?" he asked. What did *I* want to do? No—there wasn't even a question. I knew I had to marry Ant. But the fact that he cared enough to ask me... My heart swelled with even more love for this man. "My parents are insistent that I marry this year, but, Pen, they forced your sister. I won't have them force you."

I brought both of my hands up to hold his face, looking him in the eyes. "They forced you too. What do *you* want?"

As he searched my face, such earnestness on his, he nodded once, took in a breath, and said, "I think we should do it."

A little piece of my heart broke from those words because I knew marrying me amounted to nothing more than Stanton McCain doing his duty for the family. I fixed a smile on my face and said, "Then let's do it."

He smiled back, a little hesitant smile, but it seemed genuine. He knew he could count on me. His reputation would remain intact.

Usually, when people decided to get married, they sealed their agreement with a kiss. But Ant had been my best friend for too many years now. I knew he saw me as nothing more than a second-rate Gretchen. Therefore, he didn't even attempt to kiss me. Instead, he took my hand in his again, to lead us back into the dining room.

"Mother, Father," he started, clearing his throat. "Philip, Evelyn—Penelope and I have agreed to marry."

"Of course, you have, son," Gerald said. "We already told you that's what would happen."

They didn't understand, nor did they care. Why? Considering that neither of our parents had to navigate the complexities of arranged marriages. They'd all met at Brown, each couple begun dating, and decided to marry. Why had things changed so drastically for us?

The one benefit of marrying Ant was that I wouldn't have to watch as he fell in love with someone else and married her instead. He'd find a good wife in me. I'd make him feel loved and appreciated, just as I always had.

Aside from the fact that he didn't love me, not in the way I wanted to be loved by him, this marriage might actually work.

Ant grabbed my arm and started to walk. "Walk with me to the door," he said. We walked until we hit the closed front door and he turned me to him again. "I'll have a key to the new house dropped off to you this afternoon. We still have to get Gretchen's back from her."

"That's fine," I said.

"You can start moving your things in as soon as you get the keys. Most of Gretchen's things are still here. That'll make life a little easier for us."

I smiled. "Thank you." Why was this so awkward? Me and Ant—we never did awkward, and trust me, every time he'd kissed my sister in front of me, I *wanted* to do awkward.

"I'm going to call my groomsmen tonight to let them know about the change in lineup."

Change in *lineup*? I couldn't exactly be upset about it. That was me: a change in the lineup.

"Do you have any bridesmaids in mind?" he asked.

"Well... I could ask Gretchen and Gabby, but that might be problematic," I teased.

"Yeah, it might be a little soon to involve them," he replied, and I even caught a hint of a twinkle in his eye. He was taking this all surprisingly well, and I couldn't help to think that this might blow up in our faces at some point. For now, I planned to ignore that line of thinking and just go with the flow. "Well, I'm going to get going, then," Ant finished his thought. "There are a lot of things to get taken care of now. Talk to you tomorrow?"

I nodded. "Talk to you tomorrow." He leaned in to press a sweet kiss to my cheek, then he gave my arms a squeeze and left. On the day we decided to get married, he *kissed* my *cheek*.

We'd better have some tequila in this house.

Since we Von Dutton women weren't allowed any emotion other than contentment, and in the direst of cases, slight irritation, I learned to express *my* emotions through the occasional consumption of alcohol. I broke them down into four categories: 1. Wine: for the everyday joys and stressors of life. e.g. Getting a call from an old friend or your '*check engine*' light blinked on and now you needed to take your car into the shop. 2. A Manhattan: Typically this fell under a night out with friends or dinner/cocktail parties. e.g. schmoozing and/or light celebration. A delicious see-and-be-seen sort of drink. 3. Champagne: Hardcore celebrations. e.g. consumed at weddings, engagement parties, or at midnight on New Year's. And lastly, 4. Tequila: Its uses included spring break in college, Cinco de Mayo celebrations, and (at least for me) total life implosions.

Don't think I didn't go searching. My dad kept an extensive liquor cabinet in his study. While the parents continued to hash out the details of Ant's and my life, I moved down the hall to my father's study. I remembered loving to sit in here with him when I was a little girl. He'd be at his beautifully carved, antique mahogany desk that seemed so monumentally large at the time. While he worked, I sat in the chenille wingback chair and read my books. He'd kept them on the bottom shelf closest to the chair so I could reach them.

That felt like a lifetime ago. I opened the door to the liquor cabinet, moving bottles until I found what I wanted—*jackpot*. My father had taste when it came to his liquors. Only the most refined would do. Asombroso Del Porto Extra Añejo given to him by a business associate as a Christmas gift one year. We were talking a $1500 bottle of tequila. And because I felt like getting spectacularly sloshed tonight, I also swiped his bottle of Gran Patrón Burdeos.

Double-fisting the bottles, I went outside to the hot tub rather than upstairs to my room. I set the bottles down on the tile and then stripped down to my underwear. No one would see me and if they did, no one would care. That's the thing in my family —no one cared, not really. I mean, unless you were referring to what others thought of our family. Before climbing into the hot tub, I pulled my phone from my pants pocket and put on mood music I could sing along to.

For every shot I took out of one bottle, I took one out of the other to not make it feel inferior. Forget Stanton, I wanted to marry tequila. My head spun, but I was feeling good because I wasn't feeling anything at all. Not until I felt the urge to puke. I tore out of the hot tub, stumbling to make it to the flower garden in time.

It was possible I shouldn't have been drinking this early in the day. It was even more *possible? Possibler?* It was even more of one of those two that I shouldn't have let myself get so sloshed. I shook my head—I shouldn't have done that, either.

I heaved and heaved into the flowerbed until I puked my toes from the inside out while Stephen Still's "Love the One You're With" played in the background. I laughed at the absurdity of it all.

Jesus—an apropos wedding song if I ever heard one. And it

wasn't just a wedding song, it doubled as the soundtrack of my life on repeat because you know, every girl dreamed of being the consolation prize.

Later that day, as promised, Ant had the house key delivered. No, he didn't deliver it in person. *Don't be silly, Pen... Why would he take time out of his clearly busy schedule to drop off a house key to his intended?* I called Nadine to see if she could score me some boxes so I could start packing. Why put off the inevitable?

I needed to find some bridesmaids. Stat.

Chapter Six

The next morning, hungover again, I popped a couple of ibuprofen before walking over to my writing desk to begin scribbling out a list of things that needed to be changed now that this was no longer Gretchen's wedding. If my parents wanted me to slide into my sister's spot, they'd have to pay for the changes.

First, I called the bakery about the cake. "Hi. My name is Penelope and I'm calling about the Von Dutton/McCain wedding cake?"

"Yes. It's truly magnificent. The bride and groom will love it."

My heart sank. "Well, there have been a few changes. I'd like to come down to sample some cakes and look at your designs."

"Are you canceling?" she asked. "There's no return on deposit."

"No. I'm not canceling. There've just been some changes that we'd like the cake to reflect."

"I'm sorry. This close to the wedding date, your choices are to keep the cake as is or cancel."

Well, that didn't fill me with joy or mirth. "If I cancel, are you able to make a new, different cake if I order it at the same time?"

"I'm sorry, no. It takes time to sketch out a design and have all we need for the cake delivered. You can come in and buy a pre-made cake from the window display."

I pressed my hand to my forehead and sighed. A window display cake? Mother and Mrs. McCain would never go for it. "I'll keep the order as is."

"Great," she said in an annoyingly chirpy voice. "Then you have a great rest of your day." And she hung up on me. So scratch a cake for Penelope off the list.

Next up, the flowers. I called In Bloom Flower Shop to find out what my sister had ordered. Roses, calla lilies, peonies, and orchids all in white or shades of salmon. *Salmon?* Why in the love of all things holy would my sister have ordered anything in *salmon?*

"I was thinking daisies and poppies, thistles and pink Veronicas."

"I'd suggest going into a field," the woman on the other end said, clearly mocking me.

She didn't have to be so rude about it. "So you can't order them in?"

"Not in the amount of time between now and the wedding. Do you want to cancel the arrangements already on file?"

"No. Thank you."

Just to be on the safe side I called every flower shop in town, right down to Frank's Flowers. Most high school kids across the tracks went there for corsages and boutonnieres during prom and homecoming seasons. Even Frank's Flowers couldn't give me what I wanted.

Why couldn't one thing go my way? I called half of my contacts list before I sucked it up and called the only two women I wanted to stand up with me, but had been afraid to call because, well... because of a few things. First, when we all went off to college, I'd cut ties with them. Why? That led to the second reason. That being, they were the two friends from high school that my parents didn't approve of. I'd been a coward who should have tried harder to keep in contact. That brought us to the third reason: I hadn't attempted to call them since I'd been back.

Yeah, I know. I sucked it up and pressed the first number contact. It rang a couple of times before I heard the voice of one of my best friends in the world for the first time in four years.

"Pen?" she asked.

"Hi Si, how are you?"

"Doing well. I'm at work—"

"Oh, then I should let you go and try back later." Why was this so awkward?

"No," she said quickly. "What's up?"

"It's a long story but... I'm getting married and I wanted you and Glory with me but this was a stupidly bad idea—I'm sorry."

"I have a feeling there's a story here," she said, and boy, I remembered right then one of the reasons I loved her. Not much got past Sierra. "But you calling is *never* a stupidly bad idea."

Sucking it up, I blew out an embarrassed breath through my nose before going for it. "Here's the thing. It's soon. Like in a month soon. I'll pay for the bridesmaid dress, but the fitting needs to happen like today."

"Give me the deets," she replied. "I'll call Glory and meet you there on my lunch break. Is one okay?"

"It's perfect." Tears actually stung my eyes. "Thank you, Si."

"Always, Pen. *Always.*"

My heart swelled. As promised, I gave her the details for the bridal shop while I mentally prepared to see two of my best friends again. After we hung up, a terrible thought hit me. What if they were ugly dresses? Gretchen wouldn't have ordered ugly dresses, would she? Man, I hoped not. She loved to be the center of attention and yes, brides typically were, but what better way to ensure that all eyes stayed on you than by forcing your bridesmaids to wear hideous dresses? What if Sierra and Gloria ended up wanting to kill me rather than stand up with me because, to be honest, I had no idea what the bridesmaid dresses looked like?

It felt like my little bit of rebellion at the time. They'd

measured for it, but my sister never showed me the one she'd chosen, and I never asked to see it because I secretly protested Ant marrying the wrong woman. Wrong for me. Now, though, I had to purchase new ones or hope that mine and Gabby's could be tailored to fit since he was marrying the right woman. Right for me, wrong for him.

Shoot—I needed a wedding dress, too! Or at the very least I needed Gretchen's altered to fit me. *You won't hyperventilate, Pen... you won't hyperventilate.*

After a quick call to Rochester to let him know I was leaving, I ran downstairs and hopped in my car. Okay. I could do this. People got married all the time. Of course, it usually wasn't as a stand-in for the actual bride, but semantics, am I right?

As I sped down the road, I got to thinking. Maybe Stanton and I could elope. Mother's reaction to hearing about Gretchen in Vegas was almost supportive when she thought Gretchen was with Ant. Why couldn't we? The more I thought about it, the more I liked that idea. No—not just like it. This was an absolutely brilliant idea. Before I could chicken out, I picked up my phone. "Siri, call Ant."

"*Calling Ant,*" Siri replied and after a few seconds, the sound of ringing filled my ear.

"Hey, Pen? What's up?" he asked as his greeting. The same greeting he'd always given me when he didn't call me "sweetheart" instead. But, like, "What's up?" seemed a tad inappropriate, considering we'd just agreed to get *married* yesterday. It wasn't like I expected him to call me "honey" or "babe" or anything, but maybe don't treat me like his girlfriend's younger sister.

Stop. You called for a reason, Pen. And I did. Focus. "So I was thinking, do you want to just head to Atlantic City over the weekend and call it done?"

"*What?*" he asked, laughing out the word.

"You, me, Atlantic City. It'd be so much easier."

"Bad day?" he asked.

"No." *Yes.* Not that I was about to tell him that. Not

anymore. That was something I'd have told my friend Ant. Now, Ant as my fiancé, I had no idea where I stood with him.

"We can't go to Atlantic City. Our parents want this wedding, okay?"

I sighed. "Okay."

"Listen, Pen, I have to go. I'll be stopping by later with your engagement ring."

"Be still my heart," I muttered.

"What?" he asked again. "I didn't hear that last part."

"Nothing. I'll see you later, then."

Well, that was another bust. With the day I'd been having, I shouldn't have been surprised.

After the half-hour drive, I turned into the parking lot of Avery Bridal Shop. My two high school best friends waited for me outside and my day just got a bit better.

Gloria approached me first, her big, blue eyes shining. She still had the most gorgeous, curly, red hair, though she'd put on a little weight since I'd last seen her, mainly in the boobs and butt area. Not that it made a bit of difference to me, the opposite, actually. She had an hourglass figure that I'd figuratively kill for. It's just if they couldn't order in her size in enough time, we'd have to try to get Gabby's altered and that would be cutting things close.

She hugged me and it felt genuine. "I'm surprised you called," she said. "After graduation..." She let her thought trail off. Yeah, after graduation, she'd gone to U of M and I'd gone to Brown. Gloria was smart as a whip. She'd been a scholarship kid and graduated third in our class.

"I'm so glad you said *yes*, and on such short notice," I answered. "Sorry about that. It's really great to see you. I've been wanting to catch up, but I haven't been home from Providence for too long and my mother has kept me so busy."

"I bet. Evelyn loved her projects." She didn't ask the questions she had to be dying to ask. i.e. "What's going on here?" or "Why such short notice?" I wanted to kiss her for that, too. We required more than a lunch break to wade through the mire of my complicated life.

Sierra joined us—and wow, I needed them today. She'd chopped off all her long hair and dyed it a platinum blonde, and she had a hoop through her nose. Mother was going to have a conniption fit over this. Ask me if I cared. It wasn't like I had time to make a list for her to approve. Crunch time. Evelyn could whine all she wanted, but I needed two more bridesmaids, and Gloria and Sierra were it. Executive decision made. Besides, I thought it looked very pretty on her. Hip and edgy, but pretty.

"Don't you look gorgeous," I said to Sierra. "You both do. Thank you for agreeing to stand up with me."

"So, who are you marrying?" Sierra asked. "You were a bit vague about it on the phone." Fair enough. They deserved to hear at least that.

"Stanton McCain," I answered in a way that I hoped sounded *whatever*.

Both their mouths dropped open. "You mean *Gretchen*'s Stanton McCain?" Gloria asked.

I smiled like my world was in perfect harmony. "They broke up. And you know we were always close."

"Son of a bitch," Sierra spat. "Your parents are making you marry him, aren't they?"

"*What*?" I choked out.

"That's all we ever heard," she said. "'The Von Duttons and the McCains.'"

Gloria placed her hand on my shoulder. "Is this what *you* want, Pen?"

"Thank you for your concern, ladies. But all is good in my world. Shall we?" I pulled open the glass door to change the subject.

A consultant wearing the shop's signature pink smock and black slacks greeted us the moment we stepped inside. "Welcome. How can I help you?"

"I'm here about the Von Dutton/McCain bridesmaid dresses.

We need to order two more. Oh, and I need a resizing on the wedding dress."

"Let me just look that up." She walked into a room behind the checkout. We wandered the store looking at the styles on the rack while we waited. A few minutes passed before she joined us. "The wedding is in a month," she said.

"Yes," I agreed.

"We won't be able to get new dresses in on time."

"Okay, what about the ones for—" I closed my eyes, swallowing. I really hated Gloria and Sierra hearing this part. "Penelope von Dutton and Gabriella Marquez? They're no longer in the wedding. Do we think we can alter their gowns? I'll pay extra for the rush."

"You'll have to. Let me go in back and grab those. They're the only two who didn't come in for the final fitting."

Sierra pinched my arm to get my attention. When I glanced at her, she mouthed, "You've got some explaining to do."

I started to sweat. I never sweat. It wasn't allowed as a Von Dutton woman. But here I was in a bridal shop sweating and—oh, no. *I won't get upset... I won't get upset... I won't get up—*

When she came out of the back room carrying two hideously salmon-colored dresses, I lost it.

No. That didn't fully represent how badly I cracked.

Chapter Seven

"*Salmon?*" I shrieked, tears pouring down my face. And I said a bunch of other unintelligible things as I continued to sob. I vaguely recalled Gloria patting my arm as she passed me, taking the bigger of the two bridesmaid dresses, and hearing Sierra's voice in the background.

"Is this Stanton McCain's office? It's an emergency with his fiancée..." There might've been a pause. Amid my life implosion, it was kind of hard to tell. "Are you close to Avery Bridal?" She paused again. "That's Pen."

Sierra hugged me as I tried, I really *tried* to calm down. For several minutes, she let me break down on her shoulder. Why had I let my friendship with her go? The next thing I knew, she'd transferred me into someone else's arms. Strong arms that hugged me protectively.

"Hey..." Ant whispered in my ear. I'd know his calming voice anywhere. "What's wrong, sweetheart?"

Sweetheart. He called me "sweetheart" in a tone that a man might call a real fiancée he actually cared about in a marriageable way. The problem was I knew the truth. All the times he'd called me that as his friend and fiancée's—or ex-fiancée's little sister, taught me that, and just made me cry harder.

"She... She..." I hiccupped. "The... The..."

"Shh... Take a breath, Pen. It's all right."

I took a stuttering breath. "She ordered... *fish* dresses."

He chuckled. "I'm sorry?"

"Salmon," I corrected myself, still crying and sniffling like a baby on his shoulder now. "This is... *her* wedding..." I hiccupped again. "Everything hers. I get one wedding and it belongs to my sister."

While he continued to hold me, he turned to the consultant. "I take it there's no time to change the color of the dresses?

"No." The woman wrung her hands. My outburst made her uncomfortable. I knew this. Now, ask me if I could do anything about it?

"What about ordering a new wedding dress?" he asked next, letting out a harsh breath, and yeah—I felt his frustration, too.

"I'm sorry, no," she answered.

"Is there a sample we can buy? This is important. I want the most beautiful sample dress. I don't care about the price."

"Let me call the owner."

"Wh-What are you doing?" I asked.

"Just a second, Pen."

After a few minutes, the consultant approached us. "I talked to the owner and she says you can have the Bellissimo."

"Excellent. Can she try it on now?"

"Certainly, sir."

The consultant rushed to the back room. She came out carrying the most beautiful ballgown I'd ever seen. An elegant, lightly blushed strapless gown covered in crystals. It took my breath away.

"Go on with the nice woman, sweetheart," Ant said, giving me a little shove. "Remember, I'll pay whatever it takes to get it here by the wedding date."

"And the other dress?" the consultant asked.

"Donate it. I'm sure there's a bride with a special story who deserves the other gown."

"That's very generous of you, sir."

"Just take care of Pen."

She brought me back into a changing room. The dress... I felt beautiful in it. It fit like a dream, aside from having to take in the bust a little.

The consultant's eyes grew as huge as her smile. She clapped her hands together. "You look like a princess."

"I *feel* like one."

"That's some man you have, there," she said while helping me out of the mass of fabric.

"He always has been."

"Our seamstress will be in tomorrow to take in the bust. Can you make it?"

"I'll be here."

"We'll get a rush on that," she said. "You'll have a beautiful gown for your wedding."

When I exited the dressing room, Ant was standing with Gloria and Sierra. "Well?" he asked.

"Thank you," I whispered, squeezing my eyes shut to keep from bursting into tears again.

"You deserve it," he said, granting me one of his soft smiles.

"How um... How did you get here so fast?" I asked, looking down at my feet to avoid any further eye contact thanks to my humiliation setting in at him seeing me as a crying mess.

"I left work early. My secretary transferred Sierra's call to my cell. I was on my way to your house, actually. I thought you'd be at home."

My head snapped up again. He was on his way? He thought I'd be at home? Why? Inquiring minds wanted—no, *needed*—inquiring minds needed to know to the point that it consumed all of my current headspace.

"I'm not home," I said, sniffling because see? All of my current headspace. What kind of response was that?

He stepped in close to peck my cheek. "Let me go pay for everything. Then you and I have a date."

What in the holy no freaking way—*a date?*

He was taking me on a date? I looked a fright. I had emotional meltdown face. How could he take me on a date?

"Lunch. This Saturday. The three of us," Sierra said as she hugged me.

"Call me with the time and place," I replied. "I'll be there."

"Saturday," Gloria said, darting her eyes over to Ant, then back to me. She gave me a side hug before she left with Sierra.

When Ant joined me, he draped his arm around my shoulders. "Ready? We'll pick up your car later."

I smiled stupidly up at him. "Okay."

He even opened the door for me to get into his car like a gentleman. He owned a black Jaguar all-electric I-Pace Performance SUV. I *loved* his car. It was hot and he looked hot driving it. Once he joined me and started the car, he turned down the radio. "I'm sorry your one wedding is a fish wedding, Pen. I know how important these things are to women."

"It's your wedding, too."

"Men don't really care. We show up when and where we're supposed to."

So *our* wedding only represented the one person *no longer* involved in the wedding? How sad. "You didn't even help with the menu?"

He side-eyed me. "What was the point? We both know Gretch gets what she wants in the end. I figured, save myself the hassle." Save himself the hassle? I thought he loved giving in to Gretchen's whims—making the love of his life happy and all that. Ant never complained before.

We drove for about ten minutes before he found on-street parking in front of a large building. "What are we doing at the courthouse?"

"I told you. We have a date at the County Clerk's Office to get the marriage license."

My heart sank. How could I have been stupid enough to think he'd take me on a real date? I waited for him to get out and round the car. He opened my door to help me out. Ant dropped his hand to the small of my back to usher us up the cement path and inside the entry where we walked through the metal detector before being allowed to continue on into the clerk's office.

As we waited in line, Ant had his phone out texting relentlessly. At the very least, he could have made small talk. I was sure he felt as awkward about this marriage as I did, but we used to be friends, and not *that* long ago. Couldn't he still talk to me like he did *before* the families dumped this on us?

Slowly, we moved up in line until finally making it to the counter. "Please fill this form out. When you turn it in, you'll get your license today. It's only good for thirty days." The older woman talked with a pinched face giving off an *"I hate my job"* impression. Fair enough. I bet I'd hate her job, too.

"Got it," Ant said to her.

As it took no time to fill out the form—like more time filling out my Brown application than applying for a spouse kind of no time—we were back up at the counter in a matter of minutes. Ant handed over both his and my birth certificates for the clerk's office to copy. He had to have gotten mine from my parents, but when? Maybe my mother gave the document to Gerald yesterday to give to Ant this morning at work? Nothing else made sense. Then, he pulled his wallet out to pay.

"Let me pay." I opened my purse. "It's hardly fair you pay for everything. You had to have spent the GDP of a small island nation on my dress."

He rolled his eyes at me. "*Pen*," was all he said. That hurt way more than it should have. The way he said my name, I knew what he was thinking. It was the least he could do for me stepping in last minute for this sham wedding. Whatever. If he wanted to, then who was I to stop him? I tossed my hand out in that universally accepted gesture for *have at it* and waited as she ran his card. After receiving the official seal stamped into our license, we found ourselves another giant step closer to wedded amicability. Despite our friendship, what we were about to embark on could hardly be considered wedded *bliss*. You had to be blissfully in love for that. And although he'd owned my heart for years... yeah. My fairytale was more of the Grimm variety than the Disney version.

As we left, Ant pressed his hand to the small of my back again. I led, but he directed us back to the car. While he drove, I stared down at the license reading and rereading it over again.

"Are you hyphenating your last name or keeping yours?" he asked out of the blue, surprising me. "You could change it to mine if you'd like. It's up to you."

"I don't know. Honestly, I haven't even thought about it. Though I suppose my parents would prefer I hyphenate so everybody knows 'two powerful families have become indomitable.'"

"*Pen.*"

"Are you okay with Penelope von Dutton-McCain? I think it sounds pretentious enough to satisfy both sets of parents."

"I think it sounds nice, actually."

"So are you going to become Stanton von Dutton-McCain?"

He cut a quick glance at me and shook his head, snickering. "I highly doubt Gerald McCain would be okay with that."

Yeah, I doubted that myself.

"It's starting to get real, isn't it?" he asked.

My brain scrolled back through the past couple of days and it'd been real to me since the morning my parents ordered me to marry a man who didn't love me. "Yeah," I answered instead and lifted my head to look out the window, but we were nowhere near the bridal shop. "Where are we going?"

"We have another stop to make. Why? Do you have something better to do?"

Aside from escaping the awkwardness in the car? "No. My day is clear."

"Good."

That was all I got. Just 'Good.'

He clicked on his blinker easing to a stop in the left turn lane, before turning into a park. He took the path that went around to the other side of the lake.

"What are we—" I cut myself off when I saw a canopy setup. Golden lights twinkled like stars draping from the canopy. A large, pink champagne-colored cashmere throw waited for someone—*please be me*—to sit on it. And there were like a hundred silky pillows in various shades of pastel pink. Pink. My favorite color. If I'd been planning my wedding, we'd have used *all* these shades. All of them.

"Please, slip off your shoes and take a seat," he offered, showcasing the vignette to me like a game show presenter.

"Thank you," I mumbled while slipping off my shoes and then dropping down onto the throw, leaning comfortably against several pillows. Ant slipped off his loafers, joining me. "What's this for?"

"Things have been awkward between us since the wedding was announced and I don't like it. Things have never been awkward between us."

"You can say that again."

"I thought about it last night—what would Pen enjoy? I came up with this."

"How'd you get it arranged so fast? I'd think you'd have to book sooner than the morning of."

He shrugged. "It's amazing what people are willing to take on if you throw enough money at the problem."

Ant pulled the wine from the ice bucket, unscrewing the cork. He poured a pink moscato. A *moscato*. Between the two families, only I drank moscato. The rest of them thought of it as a lesser wine. Something only the common people drank. I gasped softly, feeling my lip begin to tremble.

"Pen?" he asked.

"*Moscato?*"

He poured each of us a glass, offering the first to me. I took it, sipping on the drink that went down like liquid candy. "It might be Gretchen's wedding," he said, taking a taste of his own. "But it's Pen's picnic." He closed his eyes, savoring another taste. "This really is good, isn't it?"

"My favorite."

"It's sweet. I like it sweet."

"You do?" I asked, highly surprised. He always drank wines dry enough to suck every bit of moisture out of your mouth—we were talking *Mojave Desert at noon in August* dry.

"You know," he started, "I can't stand red. I only drank them because Gretch said they were the only acceptable wines."

"Why didn't you ever tell me?"

He threw me the *'really'* look. "Gretch always got what she wanted. I was expected to keep her happy. Those awful, dry reds kept Gretch happy. You had to have noticed I wasn't allowed to have an opinion of my own when she was around, and she was *always* around us."

"True. The world always revolved around Gretch."

Contemplating this, I gazed out at the spread set before us. Ant remembered—Ant remembered all my favorite foods. No theme. Just Penelope's favorites. Bocconcini skewers, sushi, ricotta and spinach stuffed shells, and even the drippiest cheeseburger sliders imaginable. I had to give it to him: The man was trying.

Chapter Eight

"Tell me, Pen... If you would've picked out the wedding cake, what would you have picked?" Ant asked, popping a bocconcini from the skewer into his mouth. He left the cherry tomato and basil leaf on the stick.

I pointed to it. "Don't like tomato or basil?"

He shrugged. "I'm not a fan of fresh basil leaves, and I like tomatoes, just not grape or cherry. It's a texture thing when they explode in your mouth."

"You ate them all the time in salads and pasta dishes."

He shot me a look and I knew automatically why he'd eaten them.

"Gretchen," I mumbled. He nodded. So I looked him in the eyes and made him this promise. "If you don't like something, you don't have to eat it, or drink it, or wear it, or whatever else my sister forced you to do."

The way he stared back at me, my heart raced and my stomach dipped—although not in a bad way. He just looked so... so... real, *raw*. Finally, I couldn't take his intensity a moment longer and looked away first, picking up a stuffed shell as my distraction— yes, with my fingers. And no, I didn't put it on a plate or eat it with a fork. Ant needed to see the real me, the me when I was alone. I, however, held a napkin under it to keep from dripping sauce onto the throw or my clothing because I might eat with my fingers, but liked clean.

"You and I have spent our whole lives having to be who our families wanted us to be," I went on. "In our home, you can be whatever version of Stanton you want to be."

"'Our home,'" he repeated on a whisper, then after a moment, he cleared his throat. "You didn't answer the question, sweetheart. What kind of cake?"

"*Ganache*." Easy enough answer. "I *hate* fondant. It's disgusting and everyone always peels it off so you're paying for something that nobody eats. It's wasteful. I'd go for a simpler design to make it taste good."

"Fondant *is* nasty," he agreed.

"And I know it's a faux pas to have chocolate cake at a wedding, but that's what I'd want. Do you remember that dark chocolate cake we all ate at that resort a couple of years back?"

"How could I forget it? I ate like three pieces and humiliated Gretch with my '*gluttony*.'" He even put the word *gluttony* in finger quotations.

"Pft..." I waved that off. "They were small pieces. I had *two*. Anyway, I'd want that dark chocolate cake and a banana cake layer, too. The filling, the same dark chocolate ganache, and this is the most important part—not a raspberry in sight."

He laughed. "You don't like raspberry?"

"No. I love raspberries. But everyone has white cake with raspberry filling between the layers. Where is it written that a wedding cake has to be white cake with raspberry filling?"

"The Ten Commandments of Weddings," he joked, popping one of the shells in his mouth, too. After chewing and swallowing, he continued. "Thou shalt serve white cake with raspberry filling."

"Thou shalt pick ugly bridesmaid's dresses."

"Walk down the aisle to Cannon in D Major."

"Serve salmon," I teased.

"Dance to 'I Will Always Love You.'"

"Honeymoon in Paris," I said, rolling my eyes. I one hundred percent knew he and Gretch, and now he and I were headed for Paris. Not that I had a problem with Paris, per se. It was just, everyone we knew spent their honeymoon in one of two places. Venice or *Paris*. I'd have gone a different route.

"Where would you want to go? If we'd been able to plan this honeymoon?"

"Oh, if this sounded good to you, we would've started in Cordoba."

"Spain. Beautiful."

"But," I went on after sipping more of my wine. "we wouldn't stay there because next, we'd travel to the ancient ruins on Sardinia. From there, we'd head to Herculaneum and Pompeii, then Crete and Mycenae—"

"I like where you're going with this," he said, cutting me off. Then he popped an unagi roll into his mouth. Watching him chew felt like watching mouth porn.

I blinked, shaking my head to clear it. "Uh... then we'd probably have enough time to visit Troy before you had to go back to work. And I got back to deciding which committees to join."

"You know I'm good with anything you want to do. Philip and Evelyn may have made you major in art history because somehow that was more acceptable than art, but sweetheart, your sculptures... You're amazing."

He always liked my art. I made a piece for his and Gretchen's wedding present—now it'd go to him alone. From me to my new partner in life.

"I need to be a productive part of this—"

"If you say 'merger,' I'll pull you over my knee and spank that ass right now," he said, cutting me off again. I gasped. "Those are Philip and Gerald's words. You need to do what you love, Pen. If I don't have to drink red wine or eat cherry tomatoes, then you don't have to work a committee that doesn't excite you and fill you with that Penelope joy."

As sweet as his words were, one could hardly be considered equal to the other. "We aren't children any longer, Ant. I have to pull my weight—bring in potential clients for your firm with all the charity luncheons and dinner parties I'm expected to put on. I'm expected to become Evelyn and Helena."

"Don't you dare. I'm not marrying my mother, Pen. We do things how we want to do them in our home. You said it. The moment we say, '*I do*,' we're free. They no longer have control over our decisions."

"Wouldn't that hurt you at work?"

"Me? Hell no. I'm good at what I do, sweetheart. I make the firm *a lot* of money and my father wouldn't dare risk the dynasty crumbling. So long as we have the last names McCain and Von Dutton—"

"McCain and Von Dutton-McCain," I corrected him.

He smiled. "Right. And Von Dutton-McCain, we've got nothing to worry about."

I grabbed his hand resting on the throw to give it a squeeze of acceptance while staring off at the last rays of the orange setting sun reflecting off the ripples on the lake. I should've been watching Ant instead.

He leaned in slowly. I smelled his musky, spicy scent with hints of citrus first. He always smelled so good. I turned my head to see what he was getting into so close to me. He was leaning in. And then, he pressed his lips to mine. His perfect, supple lips with just the right amount of moisture—and only *I* would think of a word like *moisture* while kissing the man of my dreams. *Ew!*

But the kiss... the kiss brought back every fantasy I'd ever had about the man. I parted my lips and, giving in to the utter delectable feeling, I pressed a hand to his chest and kissed him back. His heart beat like a jackhammer beneath my fingers. My heart beat equally as fast. He kissed me slowly, oh-so-slowly, with all of the heat of a man kissing a woman he really wanted to kiss behind it. When he finally pulled away, pressing his forehead to mine, I somehow found the ability to ask, "Why did you do that?"

"Because we're getting married in a couple of weeks, Pen. I figured I should know what it's like to kiss my soon-to-be wife."

"Oh," I replied stupidly. "Good idea."

"I have them once in a while." He bent down again, kissing the corner of my mouth. "I don't want it to be awkward in front of all those people."

Right. How could I have been so stupid? He didn't want our first kiss to look awkward and *like* it was our first kiss in front of all the wedding guests. I leaned back from him, picking up my moscato again to take a sip. He speared me with an intensely sexy "*What?*" look.

"I won't embarrass you," I said. "Promise."

His expression grew soft. "Pen, I don't think that's possible. I admire you more than you know—the way you've handled all this crap dumped on you."

"I lost it at a bridal shop, Ant. You were there."

"Sweetheart, *I* wanted to cry when I saw those bridesmaid dresses. I have no clue what your sister was thinking ordering that color. She loves to eat salmon, but I've never seen her wear it."

"If you were so unhappy, why go ahead with the wedding?" I asked.

Ant pulled my hands into his, holding them on his lap. "Because I can't remember a time when the Von Duttons weren't a part of my life. Your dad would've cut me out. I couldn't risk losing you, too."

Okay, so the man made sense. My family would have forbidden me from being friends with him any longer. "Was any of it real?" I asked then. "It feels like I don't really know you now."

He squeezed my hands to get me to look at him. "You know me, Pen. All our talks and being stupid together. Bowling. Trivia nights at Crunch Time Sports Bar. Green beer and bad karaoke on St. Paddy's Day. All me."

"Basically anything your family disapproves of."

"Uh... *your* family disapproves of, too. Now that I think about it, you're a bad influence, Pen." He chuckled.

"Me?" I threw my hand to my chest in mock shock/affront.

"I only went along to keep you out of trouble."

While I sat there remembering our good times, Ant nudged me with his shoulder. "Those sliders are feeling neglected."

I dropped my gaze longingly at those mini cheeseburgers, my mouth watering. "What's my problem?" I asked. "Am I sick?" I pressed a hand to my forehead. "No fever." I gasped. "Am I a pod person?"

"You must be. My Pen would've gone after a drippy burger first," he replied at the same time grabbing up a plate and popping three of those puppies on it. Then he handed it off to me. "Quick—eat this. I'm pretty sure pod people don't eat burgers."

Because I'm classy, I shoved the majority of the first slider into my mouth before biting down. The juices from the meat mixed with the sautéed onions and sharp cheddar cheese leaving a deliciously drippy mess all over my hand.

Hell yeah!

"*Mmm...*" I moaned out my absolute pleasure. "We'd one hundred percent have these at our wedding if it were *actually* ours."

Ant dropped four sliders on his plate. "And have bowls of sliced pickles and every kind of olive you could imagine to top them," he said through his mouthful. Something Evelyn or Helena would've certainly had a conniption over if they'd seen. Forget about Gretchen. But not me. He wasn't a loud chewer and never spit food when he talked, so I had no problem with it.

"And an ice cream sundae bar with every topping we imagined!"

"*Damn, Pen...* It's too bad we can't put a pause on this wedding and put that into motion."

It sounded good. Really good. I shrugged. "Maybe in a couple of years, if you still like me, we can do a wedding redo. The one we would've had if we'd had the chance to plan it."

"Sweetheart, you eat drippy burgers and you promised I don't have to drink red wine—"

"Or eat cherry tomatoes."

He laughed. "Or eat cherry tomatoes. It's a pretty safe bet I'll still like you."

I watched with rapt curiosity as he pulled his phone from his pocket, swiped up, and then pressed an app. A slow song started. Well, maybe not slow. Mid-tempo, possibly? The first notes of Van Morrison's "Brown Eyed Girl" played through the speaker. Like I said, I liked vintage things—from clothing to music to movies. It meant everything that he not only remembered but gave them to me today. If anyone needed a reason why I fell so hard for the man, there you go. Ant placed the phone on one of the silky pillows before pushing up to stand. He bent down, offering me his hand, and I stared at it blankly.

"Gonna dance with me, Pen, or leave me hanging?"

"Oh, yeah—*sorry*. I'm not used to being asked to dance. I don't go clubbing and hate getting pinched on the butt by my father's dirty old work colleagues."

"Yeah, I've noticed you don't dance much."

The memories had me chuckling, and I told him, "Well, I let it be known that I had no interest in dancing a long time ago. You and Gretch were always tripping the light fantastic—"

This time when he laughed, the sound rose up from deep from in his belly. "'The light fantastic'? Okay, *Grandma*."

"Shut it." I swatted at him, but he caught my hand, tugging me up and into his arms. Smooth move. Really smooth.

"How'd you 'let it be known?'" he asked while spinning me slowly or mid-tempo-y.

"By purposely stepping on their toes, but making it seem like an accident. I built up a reputation for being a terrible dancer. My bruised derriere thanked me."

Frowning, he shook his head, watching his feet instead of me. "I'm sorry I wasn't around to protect you."

"*Ah...*" I pressed up on my toes to kiss his cheek. "You were where you were supposed to be."

"Clearly not."

Right. Because my sister was in love with her best friend, Gabby. "Sorry." I figured I'd be tiptoeing around a lot of memories where Ant and Gabby were concerned for a while to come. Until he met a woman who knocked him off his feet. Gretch might not have been '*the one*' but she still humiliated him. Someday, he'd find hearts and rainbows. The kind of love that sent a man shouting her name from the rooftops to all and sundry. And when that happened, I planned to graciously step aside because if being with that magical unicorn woman made him happy, then I'd give him that. A good man like Ant deserved to be happy.

My heart would eventually heal. Maybe by the time I hit ninety.

"Penny for your thoughts," he said.

He didn't need to know any of that. I realized I'd gone quiet and had to quickly think up something plausible. "You really wouldn't mind if I got back into sculpting?"

Seeing him smile so broadly at my question took my breath away. "We can turn the room above the extra garage into a studio. Or forget the room—we'll turn the extra garage into a studio. I'll have to find out the codes for putting in a kiln, but the space is big and has a cement floor, and you can store your pieces in the room above."

Stanton McCain remembered that I needed a kiln for a studio. "That sounds ideal," I said and I let him dip me. As the song switched to "Don't Want to Miss a Thing" by Aerosmith, he righted me but dropped his arms around my waist, tightening them to pull me closer.

"What do you think about me setting up my office at the house so I can work from home a few days a week?" he asked.

"That way, we can spend a little more time together. You know how Gerald loves his long hours."

"Philip, too."

"I don't want to live my dad's life, you know?" he said, and yes, I'd recently figured that one out. We faced some steep hills to battle up and die on, but I silently vowed right here, right now, that our lives were going to belong to us.

"You still like cooking shows?" I asked.

"Love 'em. I only got to watch them at my place when…" He trailed off, laughing and shaking his head.

"When what?"

"When Gretchen was out with Gabby."

Ouch. Now I felt like total garbage for bringing it up.

"Do you?" he asked.

I tried to smile. "Yeah. At school, and now here when my mother isn't around so I can actually use the kitchen without being reprimanded or talked down to. Remember, I'm known to make a real mess while preparing the dishes I see on the TV."

"Oh—I remember." And I knew he did. Back in Providence, he'd popped over to help me study for a biology test one night, startling me when he walked into the kitchen because I was busy preparing us dinner, and I dropped the entire carton of eggs on the floor. We slipped on the mess while trying to clean it up. He reached above his head to grab the counter to steady himself, but caught the pastry board instead, bringing down a cloud of flour all over the both of us. We fell on each other laughing and wearing egg yolks and bleached flour. Ant ordered us pizza.

In my defense, if I made a mess, I cleaned the mess.

"What's your favorite thing to make now?"

"Still pasta. Just last week, I made this creamy lemon and black pepper linguini."

"That sounds amazing. You'll have to teach me."

Since he didn't love me the way that I loved him, the fact that we retained our friendship—happiness. So much happiness. It made this arrangement that much easier to take. At the same time, if we continued like this, my heart would end up the biggest casualty. Somehow, being so close to what I always wanted and being denied it was worse than when I'd never had a chance.

As the song ended, Ant bent in to press his lips to mine again. One hand stayed tight around my waist while he slid the other up to gently grip the back of my neck. His scent, his body heat, and the decadent nature of the kiss caused me to go lightheaded and I felt a second and a half away from swooning. His arms instinctively tightened to keep me exactly where he wanted me until the natural conclusion of what amounted to one of the three best kisses of my life, all given here tonight, by Ant.

"What are you doing tomorrow night?" he asked, whispering in my ear.

Lord help me, this was going to be a *long* life.

Chapter Nine

"Penelope, dear," my mother said while bursting into my room with her restrained energy. An oxymoron, I knew, but anyone who saw Evelyn von Dutton enter a room would swear by it. I picked up my bookmark from my lap, sliding it between the pages of the steamy romance I sat in my little book nook reading, hidden inside one of my massive art history books that I closed and set on the coffee table in front of me.

For the most part, other people's opinions hardly mattered. I liked steamy romance. I just hated having to listen to an hour of belittling from my mother because what would the neighbors think? The neighbors who weren't in my room watching me read? I couldn't tell you.

"Yes?" I asked, trying to move this thing along.

"I need you to join me for lunch at the club. I'd like to introduce you to some of the women on the charity board."

Oh, joy of joys. I looked down at the comfortable high-waisted shorts and T-shirt I wore. Then my mother dropped her gaze there, too. "Wear the yellow A-line. It's perfect for a summer day."

"Yellow makes me look like a tomato. I don't have the skin tone for it."

"Gretchen always—"

"I'm not Gretchen, Mother. I'm Penelope. Gretchen's sparkling blue eyes are a cool tone. They make the yellow pop. My brown eyes are too warm." All made up. I just didn't want to wear the yellow dress. Yellow and I weren't friends.

My mother swallowed hard. The show of emotion had nothing to do with her daughter taking off to elope and everything to do with starting over with the replacement. I agreed to marry Ant. I wasn't putting on the damn yellow dress. Not tonight. Not ever.

"*Fine.*" She waved her hand in the air flippantly. "Just not the pink. It makes you look too innocent and easily walked all over."

"I'll wear the lime. It's still a citrus."

She rolled her eyes at me. "I'll never understand why you insist on wearing used clothing. You're a Von Dutton. Von Duttons don't wear" —She wrinkled her nose— "*Used* clothing."

"Vintage, mother. Vintage. Just like you," I replied with a head tilt, fluttering my lashes and everything. Since I'd been back, goading her had easily become the best part of my day.

"Where did I go wrong?" she muttered under her breath before sighing then squaring her shoulders and stating boldly, "We leave in twenty minutes. Don't waste any of them."

Well then. I think we *almost* had a moment.

"Sure, Mother, I'd love to have lunch with you," I muttered as I stormed over to my closet. Part of me couldn't wait for the wedding simply to be rid of this place.

The lime dress gave off a 1960s Jackie Kennedy vibe. Therefore, I flipped my hair and donned a matching lime green pillbox hat, lime pumps, a lime and white bag, and white gloves. The gloves went on after the makeup, of course. I looked freaking cute if I did say so myself. My sister, like my mom, had country club woman chic down. I needed a costume to get me through, which was why some days were Audrey and some were Jackie. On days that required an updated look, I channeled my inner Princess Kate. She had style, she had class and for a royal, one could definitely call her badass.

In exactly twenty-two minutes—okay, so I had to wait for my curler to heat up—I met my mother at the base of the stairs.

Evelyn crossed her arms over her chest and shook her head. "The hair? The hat and gloves? Why couldn't you have stuck with just the dress, Pen?"

"Because what would you have to complain about if I did?"

She scowled at me.

I smiled sarcastically sweetly at her. "I do it out of love, Mother."

Predictably, she rolled her eyes, flipped her hand out, and huffed out a breath. "Let's just go."

Point to Pen.

My mother drove a white Mercedes sedan. I often thought if it became fashionable again, she'd employ a chauffeur to drive her around everywhere she went. Thank goodness, for most occasions, unless you were some kind of up-your-own-ass celebrity, you drove yourself.

Once we reached the country club, she drove directly up to the front, where the valet helped her out of the driver's seat. I helped myself out. The doormen held the doors open for us.

The woman *strutted* in. Oh yes, strutted. This was where she shined. Me? I followed closely behind but lost a bit of my earlier bravado when we reached the table full of catty socialites. The women stood from their seats.

"Evelyn," they greeted in unison, all in that same Mrs. Howell voice as my mother, and my mother moved from person to person giving and receiving cheek kisses.

I stayed back admiring her smudge-proof, long-lasting pink lipstick until she finished with the last kiss and gestured to me. "You all remember my daughter, Penelope."

And that was my cue. I forced a smile, though I made it look completely natural—*the Academy Award goes to...*—and dipped my chin at each woman.

A waiter pulled a chair out for each of us. My mother sat, situating herself first before I sat down next to her and tugged off my gloves, stuffing them inside my bag, which I set on the floor next to my feet. Then I waited for my glass of ice water, which, thankfully, he didn't take too long to deliver.

Every woman at our table picked up a menu, mock-perusing it because in the end not one of them would order anything but a salad, exactly as I was expected to do. Salad. The only acceptable meal for a ladies' luncheon.

"So, tell us, Penelope," Mrs. Staunton, the blonde, helmet-haired socialite whose actual name was Honey, said. I looked her way. "You graduated from Brown?"

I shook my head. "Yes."

"Her degree is in art history," my mother added. "I thought she'd be perfect for the arts endowment committee. Since Cricket and Lamal moved to California, we need a new member."

"And where is Gretchen today?" Tandy, Mrs. Clemson, asked through her too-dark red lips. Tandy only wore black and white. She always reminded me of a quasi-evil version of Cruella de Vil.

My mother's upper lip drew into a tight, pursed line as she cut a glance to Helena. "She's out of town at the moment."

"I suppose if I'd dumped *my* fiancé a month before the wedding, I'd leave town, too." That came from Zsa Zsa, a platinum blonde who tried desperately to channel her inner twenty-two-year-old outwardly, but never quite... Everyone in my parents' circles knew her husband, Howard Marshall, had a wandering eye and a roaming hand. He'd probably bedded half the women at this table at one point or another while their husbands were out of town on business or golfing trips, a.k.a. screwing their sugar babies or high-class call girls.

A vein bulged in my soon-to-be mother-in-law's forehead and rather than have her keel over, I surprisingly found myself sticking my nose into their tête-à-tête. Stupid, stupid, stupid Penelope, but both Helena and Ant deserved better than to be the subject of ugly gossip. Especially Ant.

"They'd been dating a very long time," I said. "Marriage seemed the next logical step, but they both came to realize that their relationship had run its course and decided to part ways. It's as simple as that."

"Lucky for you, right, *Penelope*?" Zsa Zsa enunciated each syllable of my name as if having her mic drop moment. "It's not like you haven't always followed poor Stanton around like a puppy dog."

Ouch. That hurt. Once again, I schooled my expression. "Stanton and I have always been friends. I think it's good to start a marriage with friendship, don't you, Zsa Zsa? Otherwise, you're just a trophy bride. But everyone knows that if you don't buff out the dents and tarnish regularly, the trophy gets relegated to a shelf in the garage." Then I glanced pointedly at her. "But in the end, it doesn't really matter because no matter how shiny you try to make yourself, you're still *old* and find yourself replaced by an even shinier, new trophy."

Evelyn's jaw tightened, but I swore I heard Helena cover up her laugh with a cough. I hated being that person, lowering myself to Zsa Zsa's level. I liked to think of myself as better than that. This, right here, was one of the millions of reasons I didn't want the socialite life. The thought of losing myself scared me to no end.

Lunch today with the ladies made me long for this Saturday's lunch with Sierra and Gloria. My mother would never allow me to have them over for dinner because they simply didn't reside in the right tax bracket. But once I moved into Ant's house, we were having a cookout in the backyard with the stickiest BBQ chicken imaginable, beers or hard ciders, and s'mores.

Oh my goodness, Ant would love that. Not a fork in sight. I smiled, lost in my thoughts while we each gave our salad orders. I planned a menu while we waited for the food and I imagined creating platters for the feast in my own studio when they arrived with our food. My imagination proved so much better than real life.

While taking a bite of my Cobb salad, I vaguely registered someone asking, "What do you think, Penelope?"

Evelyn bumped my elbow and I startled, swallowing the bite down hard. "I'm sorry?" I said, covering my mouth. Apparently, someone *did* ask.

"The Art Endowment?" Mrs. Staunton said with restrained annoyance.

"Oh, *um*—Children need art in their lives. All people need art in their lives, but it's crucial to start them off young to foster that love," I replied. A wave of head nods circled the table so I must have answered her correctly.

Far too soon, however, they moved past that subject and I found myself counting the ridges on my lettuce leaves for entertainment.

For three hours, I remained quiet, pretending to smile. My cheek muscles seized up from holding the unnatural countenance. Okay, not literally, but it certainly felt like it when I was finally able to drop the façade. I moved my jaw around to work out the kinks while we waited for the valet to bring the car around until my mother leaned in to whisper, "For goodness sake, Penelope. Quit fidgeting."

I internally sighed while fighting the urge to keep manipulating my mouth.

"Tomorrow, you'll join me at the D.I.A. I have an appointment with the director," she said and part of me got excited about the opportunity to make that connection. The problem for me arose because my name would forever be associated with Evelyn von Dutton. The director of the Detroit Institute of Arts might love my mother or he might simply put up with her because going against her could cost a person dearly. And if that were the case, if she ever stepped down from the endowment board, where would that leave me?

"That sounds lovely, Mother," I lied.

The valet pulled the car up and hopped out, handing my mother the keys. Once we were buckled in and on our way, she said, "I'm hosting a dinner party for your father's associates. He's looking to expand into India. Mr. Agarwal will be the guest of honor."

"That sounds nice."

"Gerald and Stanton will be there as an incentive for Mr. Agarwal to let the expansion happen. You will help me organize the dinner so you'll be equipped to host your own dinners. It's an important role, helping your husband advance his career."

Joy.

Welcome to the 1950s.

"We'll meet with the kitchen staff as soon as we get home. I'll show you all of my files. They're very convenient."

Three hours later, I was neck-deep in computer files. Guest lists, seating charts, food allergies. This person was never seated next to that person. Where left-handers sat compared to where the right-handers sat to keep arms from bumping. My eyes had crossed from staring at the screen for so long when my phone lit up with Ant's name.

"Hey?" I answered.

"Have plans tonight?" he asked.

"No... why?"

"I'm meeting an old friend for dinner and wanted you to come along."

"Do I know this friend?" As we'd grown up together, I doubted he had any friends I hadn't met at one time or another.

"Yeah. Do you remember Pete Rutherford?"

"Pete? Yes," I said. Pete Rutherford had been a friend of Ant's at Brown. From Oklahoma, maybe—or somewhere in the southwest. "He just stopped coming around."

"He told Gretch she was up her own ass."

"Ah... That would do it."

"And it did. But he's a good man, standing up with me as my best man."

"Aren't you afraid he'll think the same about me?"

Ant actually laughed into the line. "Pen, he *never* thought that about you. Probably because you're not."

Right. I'm not. I know I'm not, but guilt by association and all that, so it felt nice to hear. "Where are we going?"

"It's a surprise. Dress very casual. Is six okay?"

"For?"

"Me to pick you up?"

"You don't have to go out of your way, Ant. I can meet—"

"Pen, is six okay?"

"Six is fine. I won't keep you waiting."

"Great. See you then, sweetheart," he said before hanging up.

I supposed he was taking me someplace that Gretchen wouldn't have stepped foot in. So someplace fun. Otherwise, why such secrecy?

Anywhere he planned to take me was out of the way if he came to pick me up at my parents' place. I started closing down the computer. Maybe he had some wedding updates that he wanted to talk with me about before meeting Pete. Oh, it could be about my dress. I hoped there weren't any problems with getting it altered.

Please let there not have been any problems.

Chapter Ten

With a thousand and fifty "what if"s swirling through my head, I walked upstairs to my room. Ant said to dress "very casual." Since the lime green outfit didn't fit the criteria, I stripped down, hanging the dress in my "needs to be dry cleaned" closet, then wet my hair to get the waves back, and wiped off my makeup. I pulled my wavy hair up in a ponytail and did light, natural makeup. Lastly, I dressed in my black jeans, the softest white V-neck T-shirt in the world, and my black ballet flats. Tiny silver hoops completed the look. Well, that and the small boho purse I slung around my body. Ant wanted casual. He got casual.

Now, I just had to get out of the house without my mother seeing me in this outfit. After spending the whole day with her, I just didn't have it in me to listen to her lectures about my clothing. *"What would Stanton think?" "He told me to dress like this." "Really, Penelope, you need to put your foot down early..."* yada, yada, yada.

Sneaking around made me feel like a teenager again. I listened at the foot of my stairs to hear if anyone was coming. When I heard nothing, I crept down each step, pausing to look around the base of the banister. Then I dashed for the front door. Could anyone say ridiculous? I was a grown adult having to sneak around my mother to see the man *she*'d arranged for me to marry.

Since I made sure to time my escape, I only waited about five minutes before he pulled up in front of the house. I opened the door, hopping in. Ant in a business suit made me drool. Ant looking all casual and comfortable in a pair of fitted blue jeans and a short-sleeved navy blue T-shirt that gave delectable hints of the body underneath, not to mention showing off those arms that had me melting when we danced last night, well, that was nothing short of a revelation. He eyed me up and down, causing me to feel a little self-conscious.

"What?" I asked, patting my ponytail down in the back to tame it. "You said very casual."

"Nothing, Pen. You look amazing."

My cheeks heated and I glanced down at my lap to keep him from seeing my embarrassment. "Thanks," I whispered. Although Ant put a stop to any embarrassment by leaning over the center console. He gently gripped my chin to lift my face so our noses almost touched and I looked directly into his storming, gray eyes. My heart sped up with him this close.

"You've always been beautiful, Pen," he said before he made the space between us disappear as he pressed his lips to mine. Then my heart didn't race. It stopped altogether. I brought my hand up to cover the one he still used to hold my cheek as I drank in all the sensations.

With every kiss, Ant granted my most secret wishes and biggest heartbreak because he made those kisses feel real, even if we both knew these were consolation kisses from a man being forced to marry so as not to embarrass the families any further than my sister already had. In the circles we ran in, they took embarrassment seriously.

I had to give it to the man, yet again, he continued trying for us—trying to navigate us away from the awkwardness of two friends being told they had to spend their most productive years as husband and wife. In every sense of the word. I figured he'd want me to have my own room and he'd have his, but we were still expected to produce golden heirs. At least one for each of my last names. Unless I secretly went through IVF, we were expected to procure them the old-fashioned way. I pictured my mother hiring servants whose only job was to throw rose petals on the path before our child walked it. I wouldn't put it past her. That was how much our parents wanted our families joined. Uh... the 1500s called. They'd like their antiquated aristocratic belief systems back.

As the kiss drew to an end, I opened my eyes and there he was, still cupping my cheek, searching my face. I smiled. "You're very good at that," I said, sighing.

He snickered. "Thanks. I try." Then Ant regrettably moved back over to his side of the vehicle, putting it into gear, and off we went on this secret adventure.

It took us about an hour to reach our destination. We passed the sprawling estates, driving into an area I rarely got around to visiting, filled with middle-class houses and stores. He turned into the parking lot of Starburst Lanes and I couldn't hide the smile that spread across my face if I'd wanted to.

The last time I'd been bowling, I still lived in my apartment in Providence. I gasped, clapping my hands once in excitement. "*Ant!* I haven't been bowling since I graduated."

"Neither have I," he answered and that made me sad for him because Ant graduated two *years* ago, not the measly *months* I'd had to go without. He gestured with his head toward the building. "Come on, let's go in."

I climbed out and met him at the front of the car. He dropped his hand to the small of my back to get us going. Inside, the lights were dimmed to allow all the vibrant yellow, pink, blue, and green neon to take center stage, alongside the black lights that made my white T-shirt glow an otherworldly shade of not-quite-white and not-quite-blue. The sound of bowling balls cracking against the pins echoed above the music playing a heavy, rocking, bowling lane classic, "Pour Some Sugar on Me," overhead.

And the smell… Beer, sweat, fried foods, and fun. Oh, the scandal if Evelyn ever found out we'd come here. And I could already hear Helena in my head, "What were you thinking taking your fiancée to such a dirty establishment?"

He leaned in. "Pete's over there," he said, pointing out his old friend. I nodded, recognizing the sexy ginger right away, and started over for his table.

Pete stood in a very gentlemanly fashion when I reached him, greeting me with a friendly hug. The man still looked as handsome as I remembered—friendly, hazel eyes, strong jaw, and pleasant, usually smiling lips—yet even up here in industrialized, urban Michigan, you couldn't take the cowboy out of him. Wearing his regulation uniform of a cowboy hat, boots, a brick-colored T-shirt, and jeans, complete with a stamped belt and giant silver-plated belt buckle, he nodded at me. "Pen, you look great," he said, then tacked a, "Can I still call you 'Pen'?" at the end.

I smiled. "It's my name, so I think that's fine. How are you?"

"Doing well," he answered in his southwestern drawl, just as I felt Ant come up behind me close. So close that he pressed the front of his body to the back of mine. "*Ant*," Pete said, greeting him. The nickname I'd given him picked up momentum and stuck in college with everyone not my sister because it seemed more him.

"Have a seat, sweetheart," Ant whispered in my ear as he pulled a chair out for me. He dropped down into the one next to me. "Glad you could make it, man," he said to Pete.

"You kidding me? I wouldn't have missed this wedding for anything."

Panic seized me and I turned to my fiancé, who sat smiling. "Does he know—"

"Pete knows everything," he answered. "Trust me. It's all good." No matter the circumstance of our affianced arrangement, I trusted Ant to never lead me astray, thus, with his assurance I relaxed. "You want a beer?" he asked me then.

"Beer sounds great." Beer and bowling? I pictured myself back in Providence at a time when life was less complicated.

"I got a pitcher coming," Pete said. "And every greasy, fried food on the menu."

"So... mushrooms?" I asked hopefully.

"You think Ant here would let me forget Pen's fried mushrooms and ranch dressing?"

I whipped my head to look at Ant, shocked.

"Known you a long time, sweetheart," Ant answered. And yeah, totally true.

"But, um... I'm wearing ballet flats." I hated to point out the obvious, but I wasn't about to stick my feet in those old, stinky rented bowling shoes. "I only wore nylon footies."

"They sell socks here." Ant draped his arm around my chair but I shot up from it like an idiot, causing Ant to drop his arm. If they sold socks here, then game on!

"Be prepared, losers," I teased. The men laughed indulgently, smiling as they stood to join me. We walked up to the counter. Since Pete put in the food order, Ant paid for the games and my socks. It took me three tries to find a pair of shoes that fit my feet. The first two pairs flopped like clown shoes. I looked ridiculous and I didn't care one bit. The laughter and ease of being around these men made it all worthwhile.

The three of us picked a ball and walked over to our lane. The food arrived. We sat down to stuff our faces a little first. Fried food tasted best when mouth-searingly hot. I poured each of us a glass of beer from the pitcher.

"Where are you at now?" I asked Pete while popping a deep-fried mushroom in my mouth, savoring the artery-clogging goodness as I chewed.

"Back home in Oklahoma. My uncle retired, so now that I've graduated, I've taken over as the chief financial officer of the family ranch."

"That's impressive," I replied. "Not just the finance bit, but that you choose to be around large animals like cattle and horses."

Pete outright laughed. "You don't like horses? I thought every girl grew up wanting a pony."

"I'm not every girl. Animals larger than a golden retriever scare the crap out of me."

"Well, damn... I was gonna invite you both to come for a visit."

"Is that invitation contingent on me going near a horse?"

"No," he replied, still laughing. "Though it's a might hard to get around without one. That's a whole lot of walking."

"Don't you have like a four-wheel drive golf cart for the horse-riding challenged?"

"If you really got this knucklehead"—he gestured to Ant—"out to visit me, then I'd come up with something."

I looked to Ant, not wanting to answer for him. When he nodded, shooting me another one of his smiles of approval, I turned back to Pete. "It's a deal," I answered. "Now, if you'll excuse me, I'm going to kick your butts."

After another sip of beer, I walked over to where my ball rested, then lined up my shot. I brought my arm back, letting the ball fly. It rolled down the lane at top speed and I thought for sure the men were about to witness Pen greatness from a strike on my first roll. But no. A 7/10 split. The *dreaded* 7/10 split. Only the leftmost and rightmost back pins stayed standing. I instantly deflated and turned to look at them. "Or not," I called before turning back to try to figure out a way out of this.

Hello, art history major here. Nowhere on my transcripts did you see "strategic planning."

The next thing I knew, I felt Ant at my back. One arm he wrapped around my waist, and with the other, he covered my hand holding the ball. "You've got this," he whispered. Drawing my arm back, he helped me roll the ball. It soared down the lane, cracking into the 10-pin first. It spun on its barrel belly several times before crashing into the 7-pin, knocking that one down too.

"Hey—*cheating*!" Pete shouted from behind us, but it barely registered as I jumped up and down squealing like a damned fool, then without thinking, I spun in Ant's arms and planted one on him for God and everybody to witness. His arms tightened around me and the rest of the bowling alley disappeared.

"Sorry," I whispered when I finally realized my PDA faux pas and broke away.

"I'm not."

"Bros before hos," Pete yelled.

"Call my fiancée a 'ho' again and I'll end you," he shouted back to Pete without tearing his eyes away from me. "Where'd you learn to kiss like that?" he asked me. "Every one keeps getting better."

I shrugged. "Natural talent?"

"Damn, then I got lucky marrying you."

What did he mean by that? Was Gretchen a crappy kisser? As I'd been learning so many aspects of their relationship fell short, this wouldn't have surprised me. But, I wondered if he'd worried about me being a sucky kisser, too? Now, I wouldn't exactly call myself a professional, but I'd shared a few kisses with other men over the years and had a whole lot of experience imagining myself kissing Ant from about the time I'd turned twelve and decided Ant was the boy for me.

My brain flew into overdrive while Pete kept on talking. "Might as well take your turn since you're already up there, lover boy."

Ha! Lover boy? *Lest ye forget, I'm the consolation bride, Pete.*

Ant patted my bottom to get me moving. I patted his backside in return before walking back to the table, where I plopped down into my seat and swiped up my beer.

As I was popping a piece of fried fish into my mouth, Pete studied me for a hot second before he asked, "Are you real?"

"No. I am P.E.N.," I answered in the most monotoned "android" voice I could come up with. "Ant's Personal Entertainment Nursemaid. How may I assist you today?"

He snickered, shaking his head. "You're quick and funny... I'll give you that. But I'm being serious. Are you setting Ant up for disappointment here?"

I narrowed my eyes at him in confusion. "And how would I do that?"

"You seem to be taking this crazy situation too well. We all told him to just call off the wedding. Walk away. Be single for a while, but he refused. So since he's trying to make this work, I want to know if you plan on embarrassing him like your sister did."

Wow. My heart sank—no, that wasn't right, it *plummeted* right out through the soles of my ugly shoes. Weren't we getting along? Here I thought we were on friendly terms—well, on our way to friends. "I'm not my sister, Pete. I know she handled things wrong, and it's no secret she's not my favorite person, especially for hurting Ant the way she did, but she didn't know how to tell people. It sucks that Ant got caught in the crossfire, but maybe check your judgment. Just this one time."

Warning: angry tears imminent. What was the matter with me? We Von Dutton women didn't *do* drama. I needed a bathroom break to calm down before Ant got to see emotional meltdown face again. Pete—*remember, Pen, Pete was only looking out for his friend.* How could I fault him for going all friend-protection mode on me? That didn't mean I had to sit here and listen to him put down my family. Before Ant finished his turn, I ran to the restroom. Though, I might not have gone fast enough because I heard, "*Pen?*" called out behind me.

I kept running.

After getting myself together, which happened faster than it otherwise might have because of the bowling alley toilet smell, I left the restroom but stopped short when I rounded the corner to Ant all up in Pete's face. "What did you say to her?" Ant snarled.

"I just needed to know if she was gonna flake out like Gretchen. You didn't take any of our advice—going ahead with this sham of a wedding."

Ant grabbed a fistful of Pete's T-shirt, leaning in close to his face, too close for me to hear what he was saying. But it didn't look pleasant or close friendish? Friend-y? *Whatever.* To stop Ant from saying something that might ruin a friendship, I broke out my happy face and stepped out so they both could see me.

"Hello, gents," I said. Both Ant and Pete whipped their heads around to look at me. Ant immediately dropped his fist full of Pete's shirt.

"Pen? You okay?" he asked.

"Right as rain," I said quickly. "Is my turn up?"

"Yeah—*yes*," Pete stuttered in his drawl.

I nodded and walked up to the lane, keeping my eyes straight ahead. This time, I was determined not to need Ant's help. Lining up my shot again, I let fly, taking out half the pins. Once the ball rolled back up to me, I grabbed it up, taking my next shot without careful consideration. It took out four more pins. No spare. Ah, well...

Rather than walk back to the table, I plopped down into one of the seats closest to the lanes pretending to be enthralled in the games happening around us.

The awful part about marrying a man who'd been one of my best friends my whole life was he saw right through this tactic. Instead of grabbing his ball, he walked over to stand next to me, dropping his hand to my shoulder. If I didn't look, then he'd know I wasn't looking on purpose. Therefore, once again, I plastered on a fake smile and tilted my head up to look at him.

His eyes gutted me. Mostly because they shone so earnestly. Swirling, gray thunderclouds found a way to engulf my heart like a fluffy, gray comforter. Don't ask. It made sense to me.

"You okay?"

"I'm fine." I pointed to the lane. "Your turn."

"Pen—*stop*. What he said was—"

"He was looking out for his friend. Can't fault him for that. You're going from one Von Dutton to the other."

"You're *nothing* like Gretch. He, of all people, should know that."

I cocked my head. "Ant, take your turn. I'm fine. It's fine."

"If it's so fine, then why are you sitting here repeating the word *fine* five hundred times rather than at the table finishing your food?"

"*Fine*," I replied, shaking my head as I realized that I said it again. I pushed up from the seat thinking that after this conversation, I needed to remove that word from my vocabulary. "I'm going. Take your turn." I tried to walk away, but Quick-Draw McCain snagged the back of my tee, yanking me back into his arms. If I didn't know better, I would've sworn, at that moment, he thought of me as more than his childhood friend.

"*Pen...*" He leaned in to kiss me. I sighed, relaxing against him. "I'm marrying *you* now. He needs to respect that."

Ah, the consolation portion of this arrangement struck again. If only my heart would stop setting me up for disappointment.

We finished the games that Ant had paid for and ended the night. He acted frosty to his friend the whole rest of our time there, so before Pete reached the pickup he'd rented, I stopped Ant. "Go. Talk to your friend. He came here from Oklahoma for you. Kiss and make up."

He outright laughed at me, shaking his head. "Only one person I'm kissing, Pen." Then he tossed his eyes to Pete. "And Pete ain't it." But he jogged over to the man after. "Just a minute," he called out.

I waited next to Ant's Jag while he cleared the air with his friend. I appreciated him wanting me to feel comfortable with this arrangement, but he couldn't pick fights with all his friends. I mean, my sister embarrassed him, so what were the chances that the stand-in wouldn't either?

Ant reached his car as Pete's truck left the parking lot. He bleeped the locks on the door for me with his key fob and I slid inside. Once his door shut, he reached over me to pop the glovebox. Then he grabbed something small from inside, closed the box, sat up, and held it out to me.

Small.

Black.

Velvet.

It didn't take a rocket scientist to figure out what was inside the box, but I couldn't have *ever* imagined what was inside the box. It was... It was... "It's antique?" I asked.

He nodded. "It was my great-grandmother's ring. She and my great-grandfather were married for sixty years."

"I've never seen anything like it." My eyes filled with tears—but I want to point out that they didn't fall. After the sort-of incident at the bowling alley, I needed this information out in the world. And I'd challenge any woman—no, any *person* to see this ring and not fall to the floor swooning over the fathomless circle-cut diamond with so many prismatic rainbows I could have marched it in a Pride parade, and the brightest white light, like looking at the North Star. The delicate gold band was formed to look like vines with leaves.

"I hoped you'd like it." He lifted the box from my hand, removing the band to slide it up my left ring finger. "It might need to be sized, but I wanted you to try it first."

As it turned out, both his great-grandmother and I had a standard ring size. He smiled sweetly as he pushed it into place.

"My grandmother left this to me. It so isn't anything your sister would ever wear. I felt bad keeping it in my vault when it holds such sentimental value to me."

"It's perfect."

"I knew you'd think so." He ran his hand over my cheek then turned to start the car. Clearly, our moment was over.

"Are you sure you want to give it to me?" I asked and he shot me an '*Are you serious?*' side-eye. Okay. I sucked it up. Compensation for picking up where Gretchen left off. With nothing for it, I smiled back at him and said, "Thank you."

As we made the drive back home, he occasionally glanced down at my finger, obviously happy to have it out of storage again.

"We have dance lessons scheduled for tomorrow evening," he said, a smirk on his face.

"When did we schedule that?"

"The day we agreed to get married."

I might have shot him an astonished look. "That's so thoughtful."

"I thought we could do something fun."

"Like start in a waltz, then have all our bridal party join in with us dancing to 'Ice Ice Baby'?" The song might've been popular decades ago, but at least in this case, what once was old found a new audience thanks to social media. Viral dances made for fun weddings.

He threw his head back laughing and that just triggered me, too. There were few things I loved more than laughing with Ant.

With the rest of the ride ahead of us, I turned on his stereo, found the satellite eighties station, and shouted my, "Woo!" when Tears for Fears' "Everybody Wants to Rule the World" played. Then Ant and I started singing stupidly loud, just like in the days of yore.

The man might not have loved me, I mean, in a romantic way, but he certainly understood me in a way that not many did.

Ant held my hand as I bid him goodnight, not letting go until the absolute last moment. He really liked seeing that ring out of storage.

The next day, I woke up early in the morning, showered to get any smell of the peasantry off my body, as in the kind of smells that I loved—grease and beer—but the kind to send Evelyn into fits of annoyance along with a healthy dose of disappointment, and dressed for a day at the DIA with my mother. Today, my costume armor consisted of high-waisted, wide-legged, navy-blue pants. Vintage from the 1940s. My same navy heels from the bridal shower and a white button-down with pearl buttons. I curled my hair in an asymmetrical victory roll, coupled with my naturally wavy hair, and I didn't have to do much work to look the part. Then I completed the look with dewy cheeks and bright-red lips. Yes, this outfit worked miracles. I felt like a pinup girl instead of a stand-in.

As I stood in the mirror admiring the look, Nadine knocked, then entered. "Your mother is waiting." Poor Nadine. She kept her dishwater brown locks pulled back in the regulation tight bun that looked so uncomfortable. My mother insisted all female employees wear their hair like that. Unlike the men who had to keep short, business cuts and stay clean-shaven for the term of their employment. Breach of the dress code led to immediate termination. All employees were made to sign a contract upon hiring. They also were required to show up to work in a clean uniform that my parents provided. The housekeepers wore gray and white uniforms that were ordered from the same company where Hilton Brands bought their employee uniforms for all their hotels. Nadine never smiled.

"Coming." I swiped up my handbag from my bedside table as I scurried out of my room, shutting the door behind me.

Alessandra met me at the top of the stairs. Grabbing my hand, she stopped me before I went down. I turned to her. "You look gorgeous today," she said.

"Thank you."

"*Uh*—your ring," she gushed sounding exactly like what I imagined a grandma who loved me would sound like. "It's perfect."

"It is," I replied, smiling.

"It's Pen," she stated.

"It's that, too."

"We're going to miss you around here. Those years when you were gone felt so empty."

"I won't be that far. You and Rochester are always welcome at my house."

"How did such a flower bloom in this home?" she asked. I didn't know about all that, but I squeezed her hand just the same. She let me go and I jogged down the steps to meet my mother.

Evelyn only glanced at me, no comment from the peanut gallery for once. This morning, because we had to go into the city, she had Rochester drive us. He met us outside with the Merc waiting. He noticed my ring, too. No comment. Just a glance, a head nod, and a sweet smile.

"You know, I have no problem driving us into the city, Mother."

"I'm happy to do it," Rochester said while holding the door open for Evelyn to enter first, and I knew he meant it, but chauffeuring us around wasn't his job. He had so much to keep up with managing the grounds crew. To keep him from getting reprimanded, I waited for him to round the car and open my door too. I missed how informal my life was back in Providence.

"Thank you," I mouthed before sliding in and shutting the door. He got us on the road. Classical music played from the stereo. I spent the drive scrolling through people's videos on my phone. A bit more than an hour later we reached our destination.

How did one describe the Detroit Institute of Art? The large, white cement-and-block structure looked like a museum with its three imposing arches and the statue in front. It also kind of reminded me of a mausoleum. But come on, didn't most old museums give off that "*I could house dead people*" vibe?

My mother and I showed our passes and were allowed to head inside. Unfortunately, we bypassed all the art to make our way to the director's office. I mean, we were there for a meeting. I got it. But if she thought we were leaving without at least taking in the Diego Rivera mural she seriously had another think coming. That mural was one of the fifty billion things I loved most about the DIA.

I sort of floated through the meeting not being entirely sure of the reason for my attendance other than my mother introducing me to the director, who seemed nice enough. I just couldn't get a feel on whether he held a naturally reserved friendliness or if he found my mother as intimidating as most people found her but didn't want to be rude because of her position on the art endowment board.

We spent several hours with the man and by the time the meeting ended, I was starved since I hadn't eaten breakfast. Even still, I refused to leave without seeing my favorite mural. One didn't simply ignore a Diego Rivera. The thought was unconscionable.

The DIA housed quite an elegant cafeteria along with an upscale cafe that thought it was a bistro. I would have happily dined at either place, but Evelyn outright refused to eat anywhere regular folks could wander in or heaven forbid, sit near us—*gasp*! The horror!

"We can catch lunch at the club," she said and my heart sank.

"No, Mother. I just remembered I have to meet Ant downtown."

"Really, Penelope. His name is Stanton. He's a man, not an insect—and you need to keep your appointments on your phone. You could have missed it altogether. What would Stanton have thought? You're about to marry a McCain. You need to start acting like it."

I sucked in a harsh breath and smiled ruefully. Yes, yes... for the millionth time, yes. I was marrying a McCain. Talk about beating a dead horse. He bought me a dress and gave me a ring. It's not like I could forget. Rather than respond, I stepped out of earshot of my mother and pulled my phone from my clutch to press Ant's number. It rang a couple of times before he answered, "Pen?"

"It's Wednesday, are you in the downtown office today?" I asked, my fingers invisibly crossed that he'd say *yes*.

He chuckled slowly. "*Yes...*" Ant drew out the word as if he didn't quite trust what was about to come out of my mouth. "Why?" he asked skeptically. And there it was.

"Because I'm at the DIA with my mother and she wants to eat at the club, but I told her I had a lunch date with you because if I have to eat one more overpriced salad with socialites, I'm going to jump off the Marriott at the Renaissance Center." It sort of all came out in a jumbled mass of desperation strained through my teeth to keep the conversation low enough so that Evelyn didn't hear.

I heard the humor in his voice. "Let's not jump to anything so drastic. I've got lunch coming. Give me twenty minutes. I'll come pick you up."

"You're a lifesaver, Stanton McCain," I whispered.

"So are you, Penelope von Dutton, soon-to-be Von Dutton-McCain."

I wouldn't have called myself a *life*saver as much as a *face* saver. I knew he appreciated me stepping in. Friends made sacrifices for friends.

"Letting you go," I said to him and as I hung up, I walked back over to my mother. "Perfect timing. That was Stanton. He'll be here in twenty minutes to pick me up."

"Well, it's nice to see you two getting on so well. I know Helena will miss having you join us. I'll relay your apologies."

You mean the ones I didn't give? So kind of you.

"You'll be okay here alone?" she asked me. Uh... yeah. I'd spent hours at the DIA alone.

"I'm fine."

"If you're sure." She pulled out her phone from her purse to call Rochester, who'd been sitting in the car in the gated parking lot directly across the street from the museum this whole time. I hoped he'd brought a book or something to keep himself occupied. It took the man less than a minute to pull up in front of the building. He waited for her outside in the semi-circle drive before we made it to the museum doors.

I transferred custody of my mother to Rochester and waited on the steps for Ant. It wasn't even ten minutes before he rolled up into that same semi-circle drive. I stood and jogged in my heels over to his car. He popped the door for me and I hung on it between the car and the door, leaning my head inside.

"Hey, stranger, how 'bout a date?"

He smiled, turning his head from side to side as if to make sure we were alone. "I would, but I'm waiting for my fiancée."

"Good answer." I winked then slid onto the seat and closed the door, buckling while he took off. Wayne State University's main downtown campus encompassed most of the buildings around us, thus aside from guests visiting the museums—the Detroit History Museum and African American History Museum were right around the corner—this part of the city was inundated by students. "Thanks for coming. I'm sorry to bother you, but I didn't know what else to do. Without a job to get back to and not having many friends around since I got back from Providence, my mother had me by my lady-snarglies."

"*Snarglies*?" he laughed. We slowed for a small group to cross the street. Most of them had backpacks slung over their shoulders. So probably heading to class.

I shrugged. "I'm trying not to be so crass. See, I'm marrying a McCain in a couple of weeks. I have an image to uphold."

"I have it on good authority—from a McCain himself—that you can be as crass and unladylike with him as you want."

My stomach took that moment to growl loudly and we both broke down in hysterics. "Feed me and I'll return the favor any way you want."

He raised an eyebrow. "*Any* way I want?"

"Unless it's another lunch at the club with socialites."

"You sure you want to make that your only stipulation? I can get quite creative."

My stomach growled again—loudly. "Feed me or die, McCain."

"There it is," he said, and I looked at him confused because where was he going with this? "That hanger you Von Dutton daughters are known for."

"I'm not hangry... more like hannoyed."

"Well, I choose to find it cute." Bless his beautiful soul. I could've kissed him when he paused in front of American Coney Island. "Go order while I park," he said.

I clapped my hands together. "I owe you big time for this!" Purse in hand, I sprang from the car with Ant still shaking his head at me as I closed the door.

While he was out finding a place to park, I'd ordered us three

Coney dogs each, a plate of chili cheese fries, and a couple of Pepsis. Oh, and a paper Coney hat, too. I had mine on when he stepped inside. He made a beeline for me, bending in to kiss my cheek and snatching my hat off my head. He dropped it on his own head as he sat, so I put on the other one.

"I'm going to have to eat salad for a week to counteract the fat from last night's dinner and lunch today. My butt won't fit in the wedding dress and it's a ballgown."

Ant leaned over, checking out my derriere. "I have no issues with your butt," he said, smiling as he took a bite of his Coney.

"You're an idiot, you know that?"

"*Ah*—but I'm *your* idiot."

My idiot? In theory. Playful Ant reaffirmed all the reasons why I fell in love with him so many years ago. I reveled in the moment, totally enjoying his company while we stuffed our faces with Coney dogs—and by we, I meant me. I stuffed my face with Coney dogs. Ant ate at a more respectable pace.

I offered to hang around his office or go wander the streets of Detroit until he finished work for the day, but he refused. "It's a perk of having your name on the business. They can't really fire me for taking off early."

He wasn't wrong. Not to mention the man was brilliant. The McCain Group would probably find themselves in trouble if Ant ever took his trade secrets elsewhere.

Our good times kept rolling as he came back to my house spending several hours helping me get more packing done. Then Alessandra brought dinner up to the room where we ate in my little reading nook. My parents were out to dinner, thus, the cook had the night off. It was Alessandra who whipped up fajitas in her own kitchen and brought them up to us.

See why I loved her so much? She spoiled me.

Once we finished eating, while Ant brought our dishes down to the kitchen, I slipped into a long, flowy skirt and tank top combo for our dance lesson. Even if we decided on something fun, I still wanted to get a feel of what it would be like to dance in a dress. With the small fortune Ant spent on that gown, I planned on getting his money's worth.

After arriving at the dance studio, we walked in as a group of younger people about my age left. Ant held the door for me like a gentleman and held my hand while we made our way over to the instructor. She just had that instructor look wearing a black, long-sleeved turtleneck and a black flowy skirt that stopped mid-shin. They must issue this look as a regulation uniform when you received your dance instructor certificate. Every female dance instructor I ever saw in a movie wore this exact outfit.

She greeted us with a tight smile and I was thinking she could use a vacation. Maybe get a little sun to rejuvenate herself. She introduced herself as *Amaleah* with a pretentiousness that would've given Evelyn a run for her money.

Our first assignment was to pick a song we wanted to dance to. That sounded simple enough, right? Who knew there'd be such pressure to pick the perfect song? It was meant to make an entire room full of wedding guests understand what we felt for each other. So what song said I loved him but he only liked me as a friend? Obviously, neither Ant nor Amaleah went in that direction.

The first song that she suggested was that one from *Dirty Dancing*. Ant and I looked at each other and *no*. Absolutely not. We had two weeks. *Two. Weeks.* Uh... Superwoman, I was not.

"I really don't want my new wife to break her neck or back, especially at our wedding reception because I missed a step," Ant said. I seconded that motion.

The next one she suggested was "Happy." That song by Pharrell. She wanted us to mimic the "dancers" walking down the street in the video with a few twists thrown in. But that came off a bit too *fifth-grade talent show* for my liking. What did a girl have to do to get a wedding dance that wasn't too simplistic but could actually be recreated without the instructor present in a fortnight?

This was hopeless.

Who had two thumbs and was getting really frustrated because this whole thing seemed impossible, reiterating why we should've just run off to Atlantic City like I suggested in the first place? *This girl.* I sighed. And I sighed again. And when I didn't think Amaleah was taking said sighs as seriously as I meant them, I sighed for a third time with more feeling.

Ant laughed at my antics, but it worked. Kind of. Of course, she still had nothing, but finally, after passing on song after song, Ant smiled like he'd just had an *a-ha!* moment. Ant's *ah-ha!* moment got me excited. "I have an idea," he said while walking over to whisper into Amaleah's ear.

I threw out my hands in a, *well?*

"Ye of little faith," he said, winking at me and I might have wanted to strangle him just a skosh.

Amaleah gracefully strode over to her phone to pull up a song. What she lacked in friendliness, she made up for with elegance. She dripped it. From her dark hair pulled back in a perfect bun to her erect posture. I kind of wanted to be her when I grew up, only nicer and with a bit more color to my cheeks. She swiped through several songs before she clicked on something. Then only a moment later, the first notes of Frankie Valli's "Can't Take My Eyes Off You" came through the Bluetooth speaker.

"Oh my god," I squealed, clapping and jumping up and down like a—I didn't even know what. My brain refused to come up with a simile at that moment because I was too excited. Ant and I had a real wedding song to dance to. I couldn't wait to see what we were going to do when the brass band kicked in at the chorus.

She had Ant pull up some video tutorials on YouTube of what other dancers had worked out to that song and we dove right in.

We worked on the routine for a couple of hours. Amaleah jotted us down for two more practices before the big night. That meant we only had *two more practices* before the big night. One a week. Phew! I was getting married in two weeks. What in the holy-where-did-the-time-go? *Two weeks.* Strangely, the more I thought about it, the more I realized that I wasn't nervous, not really. I didn't want to muck up the performance, but having Ant as my partner, we had this. I meant that for more than just the stupid dance. With Ant by my side, we could do this.

He drove me home. Our magical night was coming to a close. Before I hopped out of the car, he took my hand. "You happy about things?" he asked.

"Yeah. You?"

"Absolutely. There's not much we can do to make the wedding ours. I wish I could do more for you than a wedding dress and a first dance—"

"It's fine," I said, cutting him off.

He pressed his finger to my lips. "The wedding is one day. I promise to do everything I can to make this marriage work."

"Me, too," I whispered right before he leaned in to kiss me.

Whoa! If he kept kissing me like that, I almost wouldn't care that I was the stand-in.

Almost.

Chapter Twelve

"Would you stop?" Sierra slapped my hand down from scratching at my head. The hairdresser used enough hairspray for me to have personally added another hole in the ozone. Sierra looked gorgeous, even in that hideous salmon dress. Her short, pixie cut just worked.

Between their jobs and Evelyn and Helena occupying so much of my time, and of course, my Ant time, finding a moment to hang out sort of felt like pulling teeth. But I loved these women, thus we talked on the phone regularly. Our Saturday lunch happened a few weeks ago, and they made me answer the hard questions.

"Spill," Sierra demanded after ordering her meatloaf sandwich and iced tea. I placed my order for an open-faced roast beef sandwich with mashed potatoes and gravy while Gloria went for the pirogies. Si had us meet at an old-school diner close to her apartment. We were talking chrome and teal and white vinyl-covered round bar stools. High-backed teal and white vinyl bench seats at each booth. A small jukebox fixed to the wall above each booth table. A white hex-tile floor. Legit vintage, and here I didn't know the place existed until our lunch.

"What do you want to know?" I asked unsure of where to start.

Each woman pinned me with their version of a "*What the hell do you think?*" look.

"How about how you've ended up the bride in Gretchen's wedding," Si replied.

"I'm sure there's an interesting story there," said Gloria.

"It turns out, Gretchen fell in love with Gabby."

"Yeah—I got that," Sierra said with a hint of attitude.

"Well, they eloped but the invitations had already been sent out for Ant and Gretch's wedding."

"Then you cancel the event. You don't send your other daughter as a stand-in."

Things got a little tense between us while we waited for the food. They worried about me. I got it. But they'd also been privy to years of my unrequited love for Ant, so my agreeing to marry him shouldn't have come as a surprise. I'd do just about anything for him.

In the end, I just had to give it to them straight. "My parents and his parents were demanding this wedding take place. If I'd told them no, I'd be broke and homeless right now."

Gloria opened her mouth like she wanted to add to that, ask a question, or whatever, but I held my hand up to stop her. "No. Ant was eventually going to marry somebody. I couldn't bear to see him walk down the aisle to another woman. He might not love me the way I love him, but at least I get to keep him for a while longer."

"But what if he meets someone he thinks he could fall in love with?" Sierra asked.

"When that day comes, I'll just have to deal. He won't cheat on me. Ant would leave the relationship before he started something. You both have to know that."

"If this is what you want, Pen," Gloria said, "then I'm happy for you. You've got me for whatever you need of me."

"Yeah... same here," Sierra relented.

My girls, ladies, and gentleman. My girls. I was never letting them go again.

That brought us to the day of the wedding in the dressing room of the hall where the reception would be held. It seemed the most convenient place to get ready. I did a lineup change of my own. Since the other bridesmaids were Gretchen's bridesmaids, I moved Sierra up to maid of honor and Gloria just behind her. Not that any of the others minded. They showed up to pose in pictures, walk down the aisle in front of me, and sleep with Ant's sexy groomsmen—and to be fair, he had some crazy sexy groomsmen.

Of course, with the way Pete kept eyeing Sierra, she and I might just have some after-wedding gossip to catch up on.

"You need something old, something new, something borrowed, and something blue," Gloria said, timidly. Why? She never needed to feel timid around me. "I think you have most of those but um... I wondered if you wanted to use this–" I knew what it was the moment I saw it. She pulled out the Diamonique hairpin that her father had given her for prom our senior year. It might not have been real diamonds, but it'd cost him a pretty penny to purchase it. Her dad had cancer and passed about a month after graduation, so the fact that she'd let me borrow it for my wedding meant everything.

"Oh my god!" I gasped, covering my mouth to stifle an ugly sob. "You're going to make me ruin my makeup."

And we did end up having to redo my makeup, along with Sierra's and Gloria's. Once again I chided myself for ever letting these women go. But back to the business at hand. The business of me getting married very soon.

With Sierra holding one side of the dress and Gloria holding the other, I stepped into it and the three of us lifted the strapless bodice into place. I sucked in, holding my breath while Sierra got a good grip on the zipper. Once she it zipped all the way up, I let out a breath that helped with keeping the boob coverage intact.

Each woman held an arm while I stepped into my six-inch blush heels. I felt like a princess of the Disney variety today.

"Pen," Gloria said. "Ant's going to eat you up in this dress. I hope you're on birth control because otherwise, he's getting you pregnant."

The three of us fell into each other in a fit of giggles. Sex? Ant and I kissed—oh, boy did we kiss. That man earned his Ph.D. in kissing. But sex? The subject never came up. Not once in the month we'd been engaged. If he wanted us bumping uglies, wouldn't he have brought it up by now?

Sure, our families expected heirs, but those things could be planned out. A range of images drifted through my head. Most of them included me sleeping in a separate bedroom from Ant—a bedroom he only joined me in when his family pressured him about children. As Ant never mentioned kids, I assumed he felt no urgency to get working on that task, either.

These weren't the middle ages. Sex meant more than the joining of two bodies to procreate. It was meant as a stress reliever and to bring the couple closer together. It was meant to remind them why they'd gotten together as a couple in the first place.

Suddenly, my stomach plummeted in that squishy, *I think I might get sick* way. What did that mean for us? We got together because our families insisted. Not exactly something one wanted to remember every time they got you naked. How *were* we going to handle the wedding night? To consummate or not to consummate—that was the question.

"What?" Sierra asked. "You look ready to puke."

"We never talked about sex. I have no idea if I'm going to have sex on my wedding night or not."

Gloria patted my arm. "Girl... you look so hot, you're definitely getting slapped and tickled."

"But what if he's thinking of—" I gasped. "What if he calls out her name during climax? I'll be mortified."

"*Pen*," Sierra sighed my name as if talking to a small child. "He's not going to be thinking about your sister tonight. He likes you, and if he has you naked with him... Just saying, men are easily distractible, and you, my friend, are a distraction. Now if *you* don't want to play hide the salami, then that's another subject altogether—"

Gloria cut in. "A decision that's perfectly acceptable, considering how this all came about."

"I've always wondered..."

Sierra rolled her eyes. "*Duh.*"

The wedding coordinator burst into my dressing room. "Ladies. It's time. Let's get moving." She ushered us out. "I'll meet you at the church."

Gloria and Sierra each held one of my hands as we made our way to the limo taking us to the church where the ceremony was to be held.

Inside the backseat, Gloria poured us each a glass of champagne to take the edge off my nerves. My something old came in the form of my beautiful engagement ring. My something new, the delicate rose-gold bracelet chain dripping around my wrist. Gretchen had purchased peachy-salmon-colored morganite and diamond pendant necklaces on rose-gold chains for all the bridesmaids to go with their dresses before she blew out with Gabby. I took it a step further for my two old, new besties, ordering the three of us matching bracelets.

As for the something blue? A satin sachet stuffed inside my corset that held calming lavender and lemon balm took that honor.

By the time the limo rolled to a stop in front of the church, I thought I might hyperventilate. But strangely enough, when the chauffeur opened the door for us to exit, this calm washed over me. Just like Gloria said, Ant liked me. He was my friend. We could make this marriage work.

While Sierra kept me from falling backward as I ascended the stone steps, Gloria ran ahead to get the door for us. The wedding coordinator, in her flowy, satin champagne-colored pantsuit, shuffled the bridesmaids into place. My cousin Sofia cracked open the door to the sanctuary and wow—we had a full house. I caught a glimpse of Rochester and Alessandra sitting in the last pew. If it'd been *my* wedding, they'd have been right up in the first pew with my parents. This, however, was Gretchen's wedding. But it made me so happy to see them there. How could I get married without my surrogate grandparents present?

Gloria moved into her place. Sierra stepped in right in front of me, and then my father stepped to my left, offering me his arm. "You look beautiful, Penelope," he said, and for the briefest moment, I thought I was getting a real, caring father/daughter moment. But no. He went and ruined it by saying, "You're doing the family proud today. With the connections Gerald and I have, we're giving you and Stanton the ball. Now all you kids have to do is run with it. We'll be unstoppable."

I didn't understand. Why did we need the ball? Who was trying to stop us? And what were they trying to stop us from?

The orchestra—because yes, my parents hired a small orchestra to play at my sister's, well, now *my* wedding—started playing Pachelbel's "Canon in D Major" and the wedding coordinator threw open the large, ornately carved wooden doors, signaling the first bridesmaid to begin walking.

Everyone in the room stood from the pews when my father and I took our place at the threshold, but I only had eyes for Ant, standing up front in his suit with the black jacquard and satin lapel jacket; matching, elegant five-button vest; champagne-colored shirt; salmon silk tie; and salmon and champagne pocket handkerchief. His row of sexy groomsmen behind him.

I'd never seen him look as handsome in his entire life. When our eyes met, he startled for a moment, his eyes went wide and I watched him mouth, "*whoa.*" I smiled at him. His eyes dipped to my lips, then up to my eyes again and he smiled back. As my father and I began walking, he never looked anywhere but at me. Proving to me that Ant and I really were in this together. He might not love me the way I loved him, but his smile said if he had to get married now, then he was glad for it to be to me.

With my head held high, I took Ant's hand as my father let go. Sierra bent over to grab my bouquet as Ant and I turned to face each other.

"Friends," the silk-suited pastor with his slicked-back used-car-salesman-hair started and then it all went by in a blur. His mouth moved for an overly extended time where I unfortunately and simultaneously fortunately suffered from an acute onset case of tunnel hearing. All his long-windedness sounded muffled to my ears. Well, until he asked Ant, "Do you take Penelope Regene von Dutton as your lawfully wedded wife?"

Then my ears cleared and I perked right up.

Again, Ant looked me right in the eyes and nodded. "I do," he said without a moment of hesitation. Pete leaned forward to hand him my wedding ring. Ant slid it up my finger to rest next to my engagement ring.

Whose life was I living? Me, Penelope von Dutton wore Stanton McCain's wedding ring. Uh—never mind. What was I thinking? I knew exactly whose life I was living.

While losing myself in thoughts of the beautiful rings on my finger, I almost missed the pastor asking me, "Do you take Stanton Gerald McCain as your lawfully wedded husband?"

Wait—*what?*

I shot a glance at Ant and the Pastor, and all Ant's grooms-men, realizing that they were waiting for me to answer.

Given that I absolutely did—you know, take him to be my lawfully wedded husband—and Ant had just given *his* answer, there was no turning back. "I do."

He smiled so broadly that his dimple appeared at the corner of his mouth and winked at me.

From there, the pastor said more words, then, Sierra handed me Ant's ring. I slid it onto his left ring finger.

"By the power granted me from God and the state of Michigan," the pastor called loudly, "I now pronounce Stanton and Penelope husband and wife. Stanton, you may now give Penelope the first kiss of your married lives."

My *husband* lifted his hand to cup my cheek and leaned in. The whole world fell away at the first press of his lips. Only Ant and I stood in that room. I breathed in his scent of rosemary and dried oranges from the organic soap he used. A distinctly Ant fragrance. He deepened the kiss to the point that I could've lost myself in it forever. But as he ended it, the room filled with guests once again. I took in a stuttering breath as he dropped his arm around my waist, turning us to face the crowd.

"May I introduce to you Mr. and Mrs. Stanton and Penelope McCain," the pastor said and the onlookers serenaded us with applause.

Ant then bent his arm, offering it to me. "Mrs. McCain," he said.

I smiled broadly, taking it. "Von Dutton-McCain," I reminded him as we walked back up the aisle together. Husband and wife. We'd done it. Ant and I *got married*. It hardly seemed real.

We shook the hands of well-wishers along with our wedding party, then once everyone left the church, Sierra and Pete joined Ant, the pastor, and me to sign the license. I almost flubbed my name because writing "McCain" was so new to me. Then we were officially official. The only thing left to do was send in the license, which the pastor informed us was part of his job.

Both Ant and I shook his hand, then, along with Sierra and Pete, we joined the rest of the wedding party waiting for us in limos to get photos taken.

That took about an hour. The guests spent that time showing up to the hall and partaking in the cocktails and finger foods until the actual reception started.

Finally, Ant and I were in the limo by ourselves on the way to the hall. "If I didn't tell you earlier, you look absolutely beautiful today, Pen."

"Thanks," I said, beaming at my new husband. "You clean up nicely yourself."

He took my hand in his, holding it close to his body. "I couldn't have done this with anyone else."

His parents wanted him married this year. Who would they have chosen for him if it hadn't been me? "Well, aren't you lucky you didn't have to try."

In a super-smooth move I didn't see coming, he shifted to hold his body over mine, leaning in, he brushed his lips softly against my mouth. "Kissing you now, Pen."

My eyes closed when his head came down and he pressed a powerful second kiss against my lips. I opened my mouth under his, allowing him to taste me fully, feeling that kiss throughout my entire body. As the intensity of the kiss grew, he moved his mouth over my jaw tracing it down my neck, then he whispered, "I want to touch you. Let me touch you," before moving back up to my lips.

"You *are* touching me," I managed to say through my own returning kisses.

He shook his head. "*Here*," he said, pressing his hand to the juncture of my thighs. He wanted to touch me there? Ant did?

Even as I internally freaked out, my mouth uttered, "Yes."

Ant playfully nipped my skin, drawing his hand down my body in a herculean effort to find the hem of my dress in the mass of fabric. Oh, but when he did, he slid his hand up my leg, over my knee, until he reached my little lace panties. He touched me there. That had been no man's land for way too long now and he made up for it with the press of his finger. I gasped into his mouth as I moved beneath him, desperately trying to up the friction. Ant moved the lacy fabric to the side so that nothing separated us. Skin-to-skin contact. I moaned out his name and he groaned in return.

He built me up and built me up higher and higher until my body couldn't take a minute more. I shuddered against him, holding him tightly to keep myself from totally falling apart. So caught up in Ant's magical fingers in the backseat, I didn't notice we'd stopped until my new husband started righting my dress.

"Do we have to go in there?" he asked, pressing his forehead to mine. "We did what they wanted. Can't we do what we want now?"

"I don't think that's how it works. At least, not until we get through the day. Besides, you have friends who flew in from all over to celebrate with you."

"Yet no matter how much I appreciate them showing, I'd much rather stay in the back of this limo with you until we need to head for the airport." Even as he said it, he made sure we both looked presentable. The chauffeur opened the door for us. Ant exited first, holding his hand out to help me. And we walked into the reception hand in hand like a real bride and groom.

The guests erupted with applause when we entered the massive ballroom. We paused at the entrance to take it all in, then with a squeeze of my hand, Ant led me to the tastefully decorated bridal table at the head of the room. Despite *her* colors being salmon and champagne, it looked beautiful with all the satin, silk, and brocade fabrics dripping in fanned banners on the walls and adorning the light sconces.

Roses in every corner of the room filled the space with the sweet scent making the entire venue smell like a flower garden.

Ant pulled my chair out but took my hand back in his the moment he sat down next to me. Before we even had the time to get comfortable, guests began clinking their glasses. We leaned in to kiss for the crowd.

While the servers moved around the room filling and refilling people's drinks with either Dom Pérignon or a non-alcoholic sparkling white grape juice, my new father-in-law stood to kick off the speeches.

"Thank you all for gathering today," Gerald started. "Marriage, as all of you know, is one of the most important business ventures two people can enter into, which means finding the right partner is key to building a profitable life. My wife, Helena, and I are so pleased that our only son has the lovely Penelope von Dutton—"

"McCain," my father called out to the laughter of the room…

"Yes," Gerald continued. "The lovely Penelope von Dutton-McCain by his side. The perfect business partners." Then he raised his glass to us, waiting to speak until the rest of the room followed suit. "To a fruitful business venture," he said. The room once again lit up with applause. My father-in-law called Ant and I 'the perfect business partners' and toasted to a 'fruitful business venture' and these people cheered?

How romantic.

My father, not to be outdone, stood with his glass raised. "Stanton has been a part of our lives forever. We have had the privilege of watching him grow into the strong, confident man sitting before you. With this union, the world will learn what we've all known for years, that with the backing of the McCains and the Von Duttons, he will lead America into the future."

Why did that sound like a campaign speech rather than a wedding toast? I glanced at Ant. His smile from moments ago had flatlined. I squeezed his hand under the table for reassurance and he leaned in to whisper in my ear. "Not letting them ruin our day, Pen."

Then, to my surprise, Ant stood with his glass. "Pen has been a staple in my life since the day she was born. She's smart, funny, and beautiful. It wasn't easy keeping boys from sniffing around when we were teens, but I knew none of them was good enough for her—never once imagining that I'd one day be the man lucky enough to be seated up here next to her. She has the mind of a CEO and the soul of an artist. We're all better for having her in our lives." He paused to look around the room. "So please, everyone raise your glasses to toast my bride, Penelope von Dutton-McCain."

My face blushed fifty shades of red as the room filled with lifted glasses.

"To Penelope," he said.

"To Penelope," the room repeated and they drank.

Well, it wasn't the declaration of enduring love that every

bride wanted to hear from her groom on their wedding day, but it came from his heart.

The toasts concluded with the final two: Maid of Honor and Best Man speeches. Sierra stood to say, "After graduation, Pen and I went off to different colleges, and as happens, we drifted apart. This wedding brought two people who made my teenage years wonderful back into my life and I am so thankful for that."

I smiled at her mouthing, "Thank you."

She winked then took her drink.

Directly after Sierra, Pete stood up. "When Stanton called to tell me he was getting married, it didn't surprise me one bit. When he told me it was to Penelope, I had no words." Some of the people around the room laughed uncomfortably. Many of the guests had been present at Ant and Gretchen's engagement party, but for the ones who weren't able to attend, thankfully, our families had been so far up their own asses that the invitations didn't say Gretchen or Stanton, but 'You are Cordially Invited to the Von Dutton and McCain Wedding Event of the Year.' Because again, to our families, it didn't matter which Von Dutton married a McCain, as long as representatives from both families showed up. It helped to know that some of our guests had no idea that I was the stand-in.

When Ant started to stand, looking two seconds away from tearing his friend a new bunghole, Pete turned to nod at Ant, then me, and finished. "I couldn't be happier for him. Pen's the type of woman we all hope to end up with. I've got no doubts they'll make each other happy, and what more can anyone ask out of life?" He raised his glass high. "To Pen and Stanton!"

The servers chose the close of his speech to begin bringing the first course for the dinner portion of the evening. Every scrap of food on each plate set down in front of me belonged to my sister. I supposed it was my fault. I'd decided not to contact the caterer to put in a change. After the problems with the cake, flowers, and dress, what were the chances I'd get to plan a different dinner menu?

Every other aspect of this wedding belonged to her, it only made sense that I'd get stuck eating her seared yellowfin tuna with lemon, dill, and butter risotto. It all tasted good. But could seared tuna taste as good as a drippy, gooey anything? I didn't think so. How ironic that my sister never showed today because she *wasn't allowed* to show today, yet she was everywhere I looked.

As dinner concluded, Ant and I were called to the dance floor for our first dance as husband and wife. The first notes of "Can't Take My Eyes Off You" played. My husband held one of my hands up by our heads as he wrapped his other around my waist. We moved across the dance floor gracefully, like a couple of ballroom dancers. Newbies, but still dancers. Then the chorus hit and he spun me out in order for us to break into this simple swing dance routine. We kicked our legs out in unison and he even lifted me, spinning us in a circle. Our guests cheered us on and I felt a soul-deep pride at getting through this with minimal to no mistakes.

His groomsmen stood, whooping and hollering for us. My bridesmaids, at least Sierra and Gloria, squealed and clapped. For this one moment, I was at Ant and *Pen's* wedding. And I reveled in every moment of it, right up to the very last note.

While breathing heavily at the close of our performance, Ant pressed a powerhouse of a kiss on me. "You did amazing, sweetheart," he whispered as he led me back to our table. "Gonna take up ballroom dancing with me?"

"We could. That was fun." If he meant it, I'd totally be down with it. But here was the thing—Ant didn't sit back down after depositing me in my seat.

He walked back out to the center of the dance floor. "I've got a surprise for my wife. Guys, join me?"

His groomsmen stood from their seats to join him in a line. The next thing I knew, I was being serenaded through dance. The first beats of "Ice Ice Baby" hit the room, vibrating off the walls and I shouted, *"Oh my god!"* to my husband and his buddies. The girls and I jumped up and down, cheering them on as they bounced in unison—or as close to unison as men with only a month's notice to learn a dance could—from one foot to the other. Sure, I was a little weird in that I loved me some vintage, well, *everything* vintage, but this—"Ice Ice Baby"—The whole room knew this song after people across the globe posted videos of themselves dancing to it. But the part that got me the most excited was that he *remembered*. I couldn't believe Ant remembered and done this for me. We joked about it *one time* as something my sister would've never allowed. Dancing to hip-hop at a wedding reception? *The scandal!* Even if the song never went viral, I'd always loved it, but not nearly as much as I loved my husband.

Always.

My eyes welled with happy tears while I continued to clap and cheer for the men.

Finally, when the song ended, it was time to cut the cake so that the guests could start enjoying the rest of the night by eating desserts or getting drunk and dancing like fools. I walked over to the table where Gretchen's wedding cake stood proudly. They'd done an amazing job, truly. The sugar flowers absolutely looked real, and there were tons of them spilling over the five-tier cake like a waterfall. Ant reached for my hand, pulling me to the side of that table, and I watched in shocked awe as the baker rolled out a small cart holding a two-tier cake covered in salmon ombre-colored modeling chocolate. My breath caught. No fondant in sight. Not a leaf or a flower petal. My hand shook when he held the knife for me to cut with him.

The rest of the guests could shovel down Gretchen's white cake with raspberry filling while Ant and I—and *maybe* a few of our friends—stuffed our faces with a dark chocolate ganache-filled dark chocolate cake. "There's a banana layer, too," he whispered. "This is just for us."

Tears rolled down my cheeks while I let him feed me. Then he let me feed him. I didn't have the heart to smush cake over his beautiful face. Not after he'd done this for me. I did kiss him, though. His lips tasted of rich, dark chocolate.

"You are an amazing man, Stanton McCain."

"That's only because you're an amazing woman, Penelope von Dutton-McCain." He kissed me once more. "Ready for the honeymoon?"

And my tummy dipped.

Oh, boy...

Chapter Thirteen

Sierra and Gloria helped me out of my wedding dress back in the private dressing room where I had a circa-1970s vintage peachy-blush sundress with a drawstring waist, ties at each shoulder, and a ruffled hem and bodice hanging from a portable rack. It went with the heels and jewelry I already wore.

We let loose the chignon. I gave Gloria back her hairpin, letting my hair cascade down my back, kissing her cheek in thanks. "I couldn't have pulled this day off without you guys," I said and I meant every word. My girls so kept me sane leading up to today.

"Go," Sierra said. "Your husband is out there waiting for you."

After I gave each of them a hug, Sierra handed me off my clutch and I was off. They were bagging my dress and Sierra was bringing it back to her apartment until I got home.

When she said my husband was waiting for me, she meant it. There he stood, in his jeans and his champagne button-down, sans jacket or vest, sleeves rolled up, and he had on his soft, brown loafers. He looked comfortable chic and I couldn't help but smile at the man. He took my breath away, and for better or worse, he was mine.

Ant held out his hand and we ran from the hall. Guests filed out behind us as we made our way to the limo.

"Bags are in the trunk, Mr. McCain," the chauffeur said while he waited to close the door behind us.

"We got through it," I said, still stupidly smiling.

"We did." And that was the last of our verbal communication because he pulled me onto his lap and we made out in the back-seat like a couple of horny teenagers or, well, newlyweds, until the limo stopped us at Detroit Metro Airport, which was actually located in Romulus, Michigan, which was a good little drive from the reception with traffic, and thus, gave us time to get pretty hot and heavy.

With far fewer people taking off and arriving at this time of night, Ant and I maneuvered through the terminal relatively fast, both of us rolling a bag behind us. At the Delta first-class check-in, we each checked our large bags but kept a carry-on. From there, we found our gate. Once he and I were comfortable, we walked to the club, which was a lounge for first-class passengers, where he ordered me a Manhattan and himself a classic Tom Collins. "And two of those wagyu burgers, please," he said.

Uh, wagyu beef? Yes, please.

We moved to a table away from the few other travelers. "Can you believe those speeches tonight?" I asked before taking a sip of my drink.

"For a minute there, I thought I was going to have to kill my best man in the middle of our reception, which wouldn't have started our marriage off too great."

I laughed. "For a minute, I thought you were going to kill him, too. But my dad made his speech sound like a campaign speech."

Ant wrinkled his face. "I don't want to talk about that. Not to mention my dad, 'marriage is a business venture...' or whatever bullshit he spewed."

"He wasn't wrong... with us, at least."

"*Pen—*"

"No." I shook my head. "It's okay. I meant what I said to you at the picnic. I meant my wedding vows. I'll do my best to be a good wife and I hope that's enough for you to at least live a contented life."

He drew me to him, kissing me. No matter what else happened in our marriage, at least we had the kissing. We each sat through two more drinks and one of the best burgers I'd ever eaten before the announcement went out over the speaker system, "Now boarding Delta Flight seven-thirteen for Chicago O'Hare." Ant grabbed my hand to get us moving.

"What?" I asked. "This isn't our flight. To get to Paris, we're leaving through New York's JFK."

"Oh," he said, smiling a slick smile. "Did I forget to tell you? We're starting our honeymoon off in Cordoba. To get to Cordoba, we land in Seville. To get to Seville without layovers, we have to leave from Chicago."

My mouth literally fell open. "Huh? How?"

"After the picnic, I called the travel agent. It's amazing what they can make work for enough money."

"Ant, you can't. It already cost you a small fortune for my dress."

He pecked my nose. "It's just money, Pen. We have plenty of it. It might have been Gretchen's wedding, but it's Pen and Ant's honeymoon. I've been to Paris. I love Paris. But Gretchen would be hanging over our heads the whole trip. So we're having the trip Pen and Ant want to have."

I swallowed hard. "Thank you."

My heart swelled with unsaid, unrequited love for this man. We wheeled our carry-ons behind us back to the gate, where Ant and I checked in with the attendant, then we walked up the ramp with the other first-class passengers.

After the short one-and-a-half-hour plane ride to Chicago, we disembarked and walked right over to board our next flight. This one, a nonstop to Seville, Spain. *Seville-freaking-Spain!* My husband was already the best husband in the history of husbands for doing this for us and he'd only been my husband for hours.

The flight attendant approached us. She so looked smart in her regulation purple Delta pencil dress and scarf tied around her neck. Her hair pulled back in that familiar bun. It suddenly hit me that we were on our way to *our honeymoon* as she showed us to our seats, which, let's be honest, was this awesome private, two-person cubicle. "Would you like help lowering the seats flat for a bed experience?" she asked.

Ant laughed. "We're on our honeymoon. It's probably better that we don't until I can get her completely alone in our hotel room."

Oh my god, my face felt on fire. "You can't say that."

"What? I'm sure she's seen and heard it all," he replied.

"Trust me, I've seen and heard *much* worse," the flight attendant said while fighting a grin. "And we here at Delta thank you for your restraint."

"I'm going to die now," I mumbled. "Have my coffin delivered to Spain."

"Please don't," Ant said as he bent in to kiss me. "I've only just gotten you. I'd really like to keep you for a while."

Even though we'd opted not to recline to a flat 180-degree surface, she brought us blankets and pillows, and beverages before leaving to look after other passengers. Ant rolled us to a spooning position, wrapping me in his arms.

"Sorry, sweetheart, I know it's our wedding night, but we should try to get some sleep." He kissed my neck and I snuggled back into him. After the day we'd had, this was sort of perfect. No expectations. If he ended up wanting to have sex with me, it would be with a clearer head, not jumbled by the idea that we're supposed to have sex on our wedding night.

When I opened my eyes the next morning, Ant was already awake, resting his head on his hand, watching me. He still held me close with his other arm. It felt wonderful, actually.

"What are you doing?" I asked with a yawn.

"I woke up to you in my arms and it still amazes me that we're here. I have a wife. *You're* my wife."

"And how do you feel about that in the light of day?"

"How do I feel?" he asked, chuckling. "Ecstatic. Have you seen you? You're hot. First thing in the morning, with sleep-mussed hair, you're still one of the most beautiful women I've ever seen. Some good genes in your family, sweetheart."

Me, Gretchen, my mom—at least we had that going for us.

The flight attendant took that moment to stick her head inside our cubicle. "Sorry to interrupt, but we're going to be arriving soon. We ask that you move into an upright seated position for landing."

My new husband pushed up from the very comfortable spot, taking the blanket with him. "Part of me thinks her timing sucks," he said while bending over to help me move the seats back. "I really enjoyed holding you so close. But then again, the quicker we're off this plane, the quicker I can get us in the rental car and on our way to Cordoba. Do you know what's in Cordoba, Pen?"

"Roman architecture?"

"Well, yeah—there is that, but not the answer I was looking for."

"A dazzling river coastline?" I asked next.

"Absolutely. But do you know what's on that dazzling river coastline?"

I shook my head.

"Our hotel." He punctuated that point with a kiss of the smoldering variety. So it appeared as if I *was* going to have sex with my husband on our honeymoon.

The plane touched down with hardly a bump, at least in first-class. Our check-in to the beautiful country of Spain went as quickly and smoothly as our US check-in. We didn't have to wait for our checked bags; they brought them to us. Seriously, I loved first-class. Then like two seconds after that, I swear, we had our rental car—Ant had taken care of everything ahead of time—and we were on the road. We'd probably continue to fly business class after this because he dropped a boatload on just these tickets alone, but I'm glad to have done it this once. Yet another thing Ant gave to me.

The train leaving Seville cut through cities and farmland alike and would have had us pulling into Cordoba in a half an hour. Ant wanted us to enjoy the journey, taking in the countryside. As all his ideas were good ones so far, who was I to argue? Until the shine of the honeymoon wore off, Ant could pretty much get me to agree to anything he wanted.

Forty-five minutes into our road trip, I was hungry enough to eat my own foot. Ant pulled off into a little town, where he found us these deep friend ham and cheese rolls to snack on. And yes, despite my desire to horde the entire box for myself, I shared. I mean, they were *good*. So the man was lucky I loved him.

Close to two hours after leaving Seville, we arrived in Cordoba with both our sets of feet intact.

What I no longer had were any words—they all left me as we rolled up to our hotel. A mixture of ancient Roman with modern Mediterranean architecture. We found parking and climbed out. I should've been helping my husband get our bags instead of slowly spinning to take in the amazing views, and I only stopped when I felt Ant's hand touch my elbow. I turned to him, smiling ridiculously wide. "This is the most amazing place I've ever seen."

"Well, if you think the rest of the trip will be a letdown—"

I socked him in the gut, not hard. His eyes twinkled as he laughed at me, grasping my hand to bring it up to his mouth, pressing a sweet kiss to my knuckles before letting it go.

We each rolled a bag behind us and we were met by a bellhop at the door, who took charge of our things from there while we took care of check-in. The staff spoke beautiful English, which I had to be grateful for, considering my limited understanding of Spanish, and I couldn't really speak much of it. I spoke French and Italian. Four years of French in high school and Italian at Brown. With my art history degree, Italian made the most sense to me at the time. Had I known Ant would one day take me here, I'd have studied up.

"Señor y Señora McCain, if you would follow me, *por favor*," the bellhop said before starting to walk towards the elevators and I didn't have to speak Spanish to understand we needed to follow him. As it turned out, *señor y señora* and *por favor* happened to be words I understood.

Go me!

I loved the staff uniforms. They wore navy-blue blazers. The bellhops wore black slacks whereas the desk employees wore navy blue for both. White-collared button-downs for all. Yes, I loved vintage, but I liked these so much better than the bellhop uniforms they wore in some hotels and in the movies. The ones with those stupid little hats. Somehow this seemed fresher and more professional.

Ant dropped his arm around my waist to begin moving us along with him, but I could've spent an hour in the lobby alone. A combination of Mediterranean and Roman decor. Large, stone archways and terracotta floors. It felt like we'd stepped back in time. The bellhop pressed the *up* button and it only took a moment before the three of us and our luggage loaded onto the elevator car. My heart began to race. We were almost to our room. The first private room Ant and I would share. Excitement and fear warred for dominance in my tummy region because I knew what was going to happen once we were alone. Hell, I *wanted* it to happen. Yet the idea of getting naked and doing all manner of sexual things with the man of my dreams scared the crap out of me, too. What if I sucked in bed? Or worse—what if I got too overzealous and clawed him with my fingernails or kneed him in the balls?

The elevator doors slid open and the bellhop led us down the hall to our room. He used the keycard to open the door for us, allowing Ant and me to step inside before he followed with the luggage.

Wow! No words existed to describe the room laid out before us. Frescos of gods and goddesses adorned the walls. Gold gilding on every surface. The most breezy, white fabrics on the draperies and the bed. A slight wind rippled the drapes over the patio door, which had been left open for us, only the screen in place to keep bugs out.

I spun around to not only take in the whole room but to see Ant and tell him how much I loved that he cared enough to give this to us.

"This is amazing," I gushed, waiting until he finished handing the bellhop several large bills and closing the door to run to him, leaping into his unsuspecting arms. Good thing he caught on quickly enough to catch me because it would have been pretty awkward if I had fallen at the same time I leaned in to pepper his face with kisses.

We laughed and kissed as he walked us over to the massive, king-sized bed. His large hand cupped the back of my hair. Putting one knee to the mattress, he laid me back until my head hit the cushiony softness. I wanted tongue. I wanted naked Ant and Pen pressed together. My chest heaved with excitement from the images that played out in my mind.

"This *is* amazing," he said, his eyes full of fire. "I'm glad you like it, Mrs. McCain."

"Von Du—" That was as much as I was able to get out before things really heated up. His mouth came down on mine again. The opening act to the show he intended to put on. I tasted every bit of his mouth while I yanked his shirt from his jeans in order to finally get my hands on his skin, gently scraping my fingernails down his chest in the process. No clawing. His skin burned under my touch.

He tore his lips from mine, dragging them down my neck as he used his hands in all the best ways, touching me some, caressing me others. Innocent and sweet to dirty and crude. I felt utterly desired in a way that I'd never felt with any of the albeit too few and far-between men I'd been with before. He might not have loved me, but he sure as hell wanted me. And right now, I'd take it.

"Got to get you naked," he practically growled. I managed a head nod before he tore my dress up over my head, leaving me in my corset and delicate lace panties. To my surprise, rather than jump right to ravaging me, he pushed up onto his knees, his eyes searching my body. All of it. "You're beautiful, Pen... Do you know how beautiful you are?"

Okay, so I wasn't BoBo the Dogface Girl but I'd never really felt beautiful until this moment. Even though we looked similar, Gretchen had always been the beauty in our family. At least that was how it felt growing up in her shadow. But seeing the wild swirling in my husband's eyes, it didn't matter. At some point it might, but not today.

"You're a little far away," I said and my words seemed to snap him out of whatever lust trance he'd been in. Ant lowered himself again, taking my lips as he deftly unsnapped my corset up the back, tossing it to the floor. He moved his hands to cup my breasts, taking one of the nipples into his mouth, sucking hard. I moaned out his name. His mouth on me made it hard to concentrate, but I had to. I needed to see him without a shirt. I'd seen him shirtless before by the pool, but pool Ant was nothing compared to bedroom Ant.

Getting a little impatient, I tore at his shirt, his buttons popping off, clicking against the floor when they hit the hardwood. His chest was strong and defined with a spattering of dark hair across his pecs. I ran my hands over every contour because I could. Because he was mine to play with how I wanted right now.

I managed to get his belt unbuckled before he pushed up, tearing my panties down my legs. He tossed them to the floor with the dress and corset, leaving me completely naked aside from the six-inch heels I still wore, but he pulled each one off my foot, tossing those aside, too.

"You have me at a bit of a disadvantage, Mr. McCain."

He laughed like it didn't bother him one bit. And in the next breath, it didn't matter to me, either. He dropped his lips to my breasts again, moving his kisses down my body, spending extra time on my belly, and I realized it was to tease me. The jerk had me squirming by the time his mouth hit exactly where I needed him to hit. *The* spot. The magic spot. My legs fell open, giving him more room to utilize his mouth in all the best ways imaginable and even a few I'd never dreamed of.

My mouth opened. I tried to speak—to say his name or anything, but nothing came out. My new husband rendered me speechless. All I had in me was to grasp fistfuls of comforter while he continued his glorious tongue assault on my most private parts. My insides began to vibrate. My outsides to tremble. And then an explosion of warmth and pleasure rippled through me.

I vaguely became aware of Ant leaving the bed and shedding his jeans.

"I'm on the pill," I managed to mumble and I swore he grunted. He must have shed his boxer briefs at the same time because when he hit the bed again, he climbed on top of me completely naked. When I had the wherewithal to take him in, I'd get my fill, but right now, I needed to be full of something else.

Ant didn't leave me waiting. I widened my legs, bending my knees to allow him full access, and he slid in. "Thank you, Jesus," he whispered.

The frantic exploration stopped the moment he seated himself and we both took the time to really look at each other. His eyes burned with a hundred different emotions, as I knew mine did, too. At the heart of it, I was Penelope von Dutton-McCain, *his wife*. And he was Stanton McCain, *my husband*. We were married, on our honeymoon. The monumental meaning behind this moment humbled me.

From this point on, no matter what obstacles we faced—for instance the fact that I loved him but he didn't love me—we were in this together. Me and Ant.

He started moving, pressing his lips to my throat. I followed his lead, moving in sync with him. I bit my lip, trying desperately not to make too much noise, but it got to be too much and I couldn't hold the sound in. He laughed, bending in to capture my cries with his mouth.

And oh my god!

The man was playing with me, bringing me to the brink of ecstasy but then pulling back over and over again. Time stopped around us as we moved together. The world outside our hotel room could have moved hours, days, or years in the time he took to get me panting and ready to explode again.

I... I... *"Ant,"* I cried before it hit me like the Fourth of July fireworks grand finale. The pop, pop, pop wouldn't let up. I tried to take in a breath and couldn't fill my lungs. If I was about to die, then this would be the best way possible. I dug my fingernails into the skin at his shoulders—the dreaded clawing—pinching my eyes shut and pressing my forehead to his, shaking violently while he continued to move until his whole body went rigid and he roared out his release.

"Shit, Pen..." He sucked in a breath. "Nothing better... than hearing you say my name... while I'm inside you."

Hmm, apparently he didn't mind the clawing. And did he really just say that?

We lay together, neither of us able to utter another sound, but he continued to hold me while we came down from the orgasmic high.

Overcome with the emotion from his words, I almost made a fatal mistake. "I l—" *Shoot.* My mouth knew better than to try to speak after such an extraordinary experience as my first time with Ant. "I think I like you, Stanton McCain," I said, covering my tracks. That was too close for comfort.

The last thing either of us needed was for me to say the one thing that he couldn't say back.

The one thing I wished he could.

Damn you, Stanton McCain.

Chapter Fourteen

We really should have checked out the sights, but we—well, I wouldn't say we *wasted* that first day in Cordoba, we simply kept our sightseeing to the hotel room and used the bed for our cardio workout.

"Hungry, Pen?" he asked. We'd been up for about half an hour, but given that this was only our second day in Spain and my legs were Jell-O, I stayed in bed for a while. Ant lay on his side, his head propped up on his hand, still gloriously naked.

"We should probably eat—" I started to say when Ant shot his gaze down to my nether regions. "Food, husband. We should eat food."

"I like my idea better."

"I think you need to give me some recovery time first. My vagina was sold as-is. You break it, you still bought it."

He scooped me up into his arms, laughing—*again*. Clearly, and I loved this part, he laughed around me all the time. Maybe because *I* was funny or maybe because we were funny *together*. Whatever the reason, I was sure of one thing—if you didn't laugh together, you were with the wrong person.

"Still worth the purchase price, sweetheart. But we are in

Spain for such a limited time, we should probably go out and see some of it."

My heart felt light, even as I lamented having to leave this big, beautiful bed.

One perk of being on my honeymoon with a man like Ant: *the shower*. Having him wash my hair turned out to be one of the most sensual moments of my life. I only got as far as sudsing the cloth and swiping it across his chest when we broke the recovery rule and he took me up against the Italian tile.

Ant and I finally made it out of the hotel room fully dressed and ready for our non-horizontal adventure.

Cordoba amazed me in all the ways. As did the ruins on Sardinia, which we visited two days later. Beautiful hotel there. Three days after Sardinia, we hit Italy where Ant booked us a private tour guided by an archeologist, who started us at Mt. Vesuvius, explaining about the eruption in 79 CE and the impact it had on the rest of the world for years to come. Then we moved to the coast, where we took in Herculaneum first, then made our way down to the ruins in Oplontis and finally, we ended in Pompeii. And by the way, Ant kept upping his hotel game, I mean, for what we actually saw of them.

As we walked down the stone streets, our guide brought into vivid detail the lives of the men and women of the ancient Roman city. She pointed out interesting facts about the brothels, which Ant seemed particularly interested in, including reading some of the centuries-old graffiti from customers particularly satisfied with their experiences. Turns out, men in 79 CE liked the same exact things as men today. Ant and I had done most of those that morning in the hotel room.

We toured the theater, a public baths, and a villa, where we got to see the most incredible frescos. But I think one of my favorite parts, the part that really made me think about the people who'd lived there, was when she showed us a stick figure drawn by a Pompeiian child all those years ago. Our guide led us to the building where we stood in front of a glass coffin holding one of the famous rock shapes, this one of a child.

"We should move here," I told Ant while walking around the home of a politician and business owner. Given inflation, this man definitely had the wealth to run in the same circles as the Von Duttons and McCains.

"I'm not opposed to the idea. Can't beat the weather."

"Or the food," I said.

"The food's incredible. But you know, there is that whole active volcano to deal with. Still, I'm game if you are."

"*Yeah*... I forgot about that."

"How 'bout if I promise to bring you back?"

"Deal," I said, pushing up on my tiptoes to kiss him.

Even though not part of the original itinerary—the one from that talk way back on our picnic by the lake on "wedding dress meltdown" day, seeing as we were in Italy, which was arguably one of the most beautiful and romantic countries in the world, we made an impromptu trip north to tour the cities of Rome, where we took in the sites, including going back to the Sistine Chapel in Vatican City, and then on to Florence. I'd spent a semester in Rome and Florence studying art history, but as wonderful as it had been to tour those cities with other students, it didn't even compare to being there with Ant, who as it turned out, was a real romantic at heart. After a couple of days in Rome, I wanted him to see the statue of David and oh my god, I needed to show him Michelangelo's *Prisoners*. So we headed to Florence and okay, so I geeked out. I challenge anyone not to in the presence of such genius.

To my shock and horror, he'd never heard of Ghiberti's *The Gates of Paradise*. Made of bronze, the gates stood over sixteen and a half feet tall and weighed, like, three tons. Before we left, he had to see Botticelli's *Birth of Venus*, which had to be the most famous painting to still reside in the city. We ended our day at *The Fountain of Neptune*.

"I've been to Italy a few different times and this is the first that

I stopped to see all the art," Ant said as we left the gorgeous city behind on our way to Venice. Yes, we became that couple who honeymooned in Venice. Sue me. He reached over to hold my hand, pulling it to rest on his lap. "Gretch and I toured the Colosseum, the Pantheon, Trevi Fountain, and the Piazza Navona, but she wanted to hit the vineyards."

"Well, I'm glad that I could give you a new experience, then. That alone has to be worth the price of admission." I winked at him and he smiled, giving my hand a squeeze.

"Woman, you're already the best wife I've ever had."

"Back acha. Out of all my husbands, you're the best by far."

"Really? I don't remember you having any other husbands. How many were there? What were their names?"

I said the first number to pop into my head. "There were seven—all named John."

"Seven?" He threw his hand, the one he'd been using to hold mine to his chest, in mock astonishment. "And you're only twenty-three? What happened to them?"

"They all disappeared under very questionable circumstances. The authorities simply have no leads."

"Should I be worried?"

"Well, your name isn't John, so the odds are in your favor, but just to be safe, I wouldn't tick me off."

"Your wish is my command, sweetheart."

Love me. That's my wish. Still, I couldn't complain. I'd fallen in love all over again with the Italian landscape between Florence and Venice.

Somehow, my wonderful husband managed to book us a room at the Baglioni Hotel Luna, which claimed to be the oldest hotel in Venice. It was certainly one of the most famous and been in the most movies.

Only one word came to mind when describing Baglioni Hotel Luna: opulent. Silks and satins, and trimmed with gold. We were given a canal view, but I'd have been happy with the courtyard view because a courtyard view at the Baglioni Hotel Luna was still a courtyard view at the *Baglioni Hotel Luna*.

I walked from where I stood staring out over the balcony to where he was looking for something in his bag. He stood up straight and I threw my arms around his neck.

"This is amazing, Ant. You're amazing. Thank you."

"My pleasure, Pen. I couldn't have imagined a better honeymoon."

"You want to take a gondola ride?"

"Yes. But *first...*" He waggled his eyebrows at me.

Okay, so we totally broke in the bed. I had to give it to us. Ant and I really had this sex thing down. We went at it like sexual rock stars. I didn't know that I had a wild side before this trip. And who knew he'd be so responsive to all my touches?

A couple of hours passed before we made it outside again. We meandered our way down to the canal, where Ant bought us a one-hour private gondola tour. As the most expensive option, it didn't have the wait times of the regular tours and we got to see parts of the city only accessible from the canal. It was no wonder so many tourists came to honeymoon in Venice. Lounging back against Ant, his arms holding me as the gondolier told us about the history of the city, I really doubted any place in the world could be more romantic.

"You look young. How long have you been married?" the gondolier asked as he maneuvered us past another gondola heading the opposite way. He was dressed like the classic gondolier: black-and-white striped shirt, black pants, flat-brimmed hat, a red scarf tied around his neck, and a red sash around his waist.

"We're on our honeymoon," Ant answered.

"Honeymoon? Congratulations. I didn't get honeymooners —you're both so comfortable with each other. Like you've been married for years."

"We've known each other literally our whole lives. Pen here, she was always one of my best friends."

"*Ah—*" the gondolier said, nodding, gliding the paddle

through the water. "That makes sense. I wish you years of happiness." That was the last he spoke of it, going back to telling us about the city.

By the close of our ride, I needed food in my belly. Since getting a little preoccupied earlier and thus forgetting to make a dinner reservation, we asked the gondolier where was the best place to go, and he pointed us in the direction of his favorite bàcaro. These were small eateries that served simple fare. We ordered bread, meat, cheeses, and a relish spread to go along with —*squeee*—Moscato to drink! We could have ordered room service once we got back to the hotel, but we didn't want to wait.

Ant and I took the elevator up to our room, where he led me onto the balcony and we watched the tourists below us riding the canals as we ate. I never wanted to leave.

Later that night, while I lay blissfully naked on my stomach in bed, my arms on my pillow, my face on my arms, I watched Ant, who lay on his back, bare chest exposed, with his head on his hands, both of us at our most comfortable. "Did you have any idea?" I asked.

"About?"

"Gretchen. I knew she and Gabby were close, but I just didn't see it. Were there signs I missed?"

He sighed. "I don't know that I really looked, to be honest. From the time Gretch and I were old enough to date, we'd been paired up. No one gave us a choice. Things were fine between us —not that I'd say, looking back on it, that there was ever really a spark. As the first and only woman I took to my bed before you, I thought things were good there, too." Then he rolled to face me. "I didn't know how explosive sex could be until you in Cordoba. If there's one thing that can be said about us, Pen, it's that we have chemistry."

"I'm so happy here with you—I want you to know that—but I'm so sorry that you had to live the embarrassment of having your fiancée dump you."

He reached his hand over, tracing the exposed skin on my

back with his finger. "Things worked out as they were meant to. No one should be mad at your sister. She did the brave thing. She fell in love and had the courage to go against the families to be with Gabby."

Unlike us, right? I read his meaning. We didn't go against our families. Gretch did the brave thing. We didn't. If he only knew why I'd never fussed about marrying him.

He said it, at the very least: we had chemistry. If this made him happy, then this was what he'd get. I slid closer to him, throwing my leg over his hips to straddle him. Ant raised an eyebrow.

"I thought you said after the last round that you might never be able to have sex again."

I shot him a coy, one-shoulder shrug. "I was wrong. You going to complain or f—"

I didn't even get the word out before his lips found mine again and he spent the rest of the night *f*—ing me.

Whoa.

Chapter Fifteen

Because of our impromptu diversion farther north into Italy, we lost our reservations on Crete and Mycenae, which I thought was going to send us home sooner than I wanted to go. Here, in Europe, we were Ant and Pen—*just* Ant and Pen, a couple on honeymoon from America without an ex-fiancée or the names Von Dutton and McCain hanging over our heads.

As it turned out, though, those names came in handy. Ant called up one of McCain Group's foreign associates who happened to be a Greek shipping magnate, an associate who had been at our wedding. He explained the situation and the next thing I knew, we were on our way down to Crete to stay in one of this man's vacation homes.

Who knew water came so crystal clear? The private beach made me feel like Ant and I were the only two people on the planet.

"Beautiful breeze tonight," he said while holding me as we lounged on the most alluring beach possibly in existence. He nuzzled his nose against my neck. And with the setting sun concealing us from the rest of the world by blanketing us in its tangerine rays, my husband pulled the strings to my bikini top and tossed the thin triangles of fabric to the white sand beneath our chaise.

"It is," I replied, reaching up behind me to run my fingers through his thick, wind-kissed hair. The air smelled salty and sweet with a hint of coconut from our tanning lotion. Once the sun completely disappeared for the night, he made love to me on that beach under the moonlight, with the warm water lapping at our legs and feet. Probably the most romantic moment of my life, even if I ended up with sand in places people should never have to deal with sand.

We took a weekend to Türkiye to visit the city of Troy, but Ant didn't want to give up that beach. In truth, neither did I, so we only brought our overnight bags.

The last week of our honeymoon brought us golden tans, the most delicious Greek food, and relaxation—when I wasn't busy *getting busy* with my husband.

"Can't we stay?" I whined to Ant while we sat in the club at Heraklion International Airport waiting for our flight home. "You could work remotely and I could open a studio. It could be just you and me, without all that other crap."

He stroked my hair softly until finally dropping his hand to the nape of my neck where he left it resting. "We're American, Pen. It's not so easy to just pick up and move to a foreign country, especially in Europe. Not without a lot of paperwork."

"Then we can keep Michigan as our primary residence and just spend our time at our vacation home."

Ant gave my neck a gentle squeeze and leaned in to press his mouth to mine. "We'd still need to go home until we found a vacation home."

"Don't crush my dreams, McCain," I warned and he bit his lip to hold back his humor, shaking his head at me.

Before too long, we were called to board with the other first-class passengers. We drank cocktails and ate a several-course meal that was quite good for airplane fare. Way too soon for my comfort, we landed at Dulles International Airport to make our connecting flight back to Detroit.

Home again, home again, jiggity-jog.

We had an Uber waiting for us to bring us home. I got a little confused for a second when the driver didn't turn in the direction of my parents' home.

"I thought you said we were going home," I said.

"We are." He smiled one of those ridiculously handsome Ant smiles that got me in the gut every time. "*Our* home, Pen. You don't live with your parents any longer."

I rolled my eyes. "I knew that," I replied, but did it laughing at my ridiculousness.

"I took off an extra week to make sure we get you settled."

"That was kind of you. Are you okay with me having Sierra and Gloria over for a cookout?"

"That'd be great. I'll invite my cousin Cormac and his wife."

"We don't see him too often. Aside from him standing up in the wedding with you, it'd been years for me."

"He '*married below his status.*'" He used finger quotes, wrinkling his nose at the distasteful comment I knew had to come from one or all of my new extended family. Ant's uncle and aunt were exactly like Gerald and Helena. *Exactly.* "But I think you'll really like Liz," he finished. "She's sweet. Has a kind heart—a lot like you, actually."

Here I'd known the McCain family my entire life but had no idea that Ant's cousin Cormac had a wife named Liz. How sad was that? Ant used to be close with Cormac growing up. But I guessed that was what you got when you married against the family. Give it some time and the same was sure to happen to Gretchen. I was proud of my husband for giving that big FU to all the snobs by not only inviting them but having Cormac stand up with him.

"Was Liz at the wedding?" I asked. Sure, we'd been busy but not too busy for me to meet the wife of Ant's favorite cousin.

He shook his head. "I invited her but she declined. With

Corm busy doing groomsman duties, she didn't want to be left alone to the wolves. I completely understood."

Yeah, I understood, as well.

"Then let's plan it," I said, now more excited to be back than I had been a few minutes ago. This gave me something to look forward to. "I want to meet Liz."

The Uber driver let us off in front of our home, mine and Ant's. Beautiful. Large. Way larger than two people needed to live comfortably. Typical Georgian architecture of this area of Michigan. Brick exterior full of white-framed windows; small, covered stoop; and white door. As I said, beautiful, but not really my style. Definitely Gretchen's style. We rolled our bags up to the front door and paused for Ant to unlock it for us.

From the moment I walked inside, I felt like I was in someone else's home. Gretchen's, to be exact. Everything looked exactly as my sister wanted it to look. She'd decorated this house, which oozed Georgian elegance. Floor-to-ceiling windows covered by beautiful floral damask draperies. The walls painted a pale robin's egg blue with white wainscoting. Antiques in every room. It looked museum show quality.

My heart sank a little more.

This was not a house you raised children in. I wanted a home. A warm place where Ant and I celebrated holidays with friends and if someone spilled their drink, oh well. We'd clean it up and move on.

I was afraid to touch anything.

Piled neatly in the dining room and spilling over into the formal living room were all the wedding gifts.

He'd given me a key to this place the night we agreed to marry, but with so little time to get things ready, I never actually made it over here. Instead, I hired movers to bring my boxes because it wasn't worth courting the wrath of Evelyn. Von Duttons and McCains didn't do manual labor. We threw money at people to get the job done for us.

Ant held his hand out to me and I took it automatically.

"Let's dump these bags in the laundry, and then I'll show you to your room, Mrs. McCain."

He dropped his voice low and I knew what he wanted. Ant led us through the dining room, past the kitchen, to the back of the house, where the laundry was located. We left the bags and then headed up the back staircase to the second floor. The second floor held five bedrooms total, and the back staircase opened up across from the master suite.

The moment I stepped inside seeing that hulking bed for the first time, I froze.

Ant turned me to him. "What's wrong?"

"Did she?" I pointed to the bed because I just couldn't be expected to get it on with my husband in a bed where he'd bedded my sister. That was a whole other level of *ew* that I couldn't get behind. Like *ever*.

"Never, Pen. Gretch never spent one night here... I *promise*."

After knowing him my entire life, one thing was certain. Ant wouldn't promise if it weren't the truth. Crisis averted, I let him lead me inside the rest of the way. The master bath held a humongous clawfoot tub that could hold four, and a separate shower. The commode and sink were sectioned off from the bathing area. Also sectioned off from the bathing area was a vanity for me to do my makeup and hair.

Off the main room, we had a walk-in closet that probably started life as a sixth bedroom, to be honest. Inside the main room, aside from the king-sized bed, we had a fireplace with a sitting nook for reading.

As he concluded the tour, I slid my hand up his chest to unbutton his top button. "You're way overdressed for bed."

His eyes heated as he dropped his hands to the hem of my blouse. "That makes two of us."

Oh *wow*—Ant and I went wild in the bedroom. There were few things I could give him that my sister hadn't already given him and wild sex was one of them. One of the best perks of getting hot and heavy in a house that was all ours: We could be as loud as we wanted to be.

The housekeeper didn't live here, she showed up for her 9-5, so when I said we could be as loud as we wanted, I meant we shouted the roof off—well, maybe not *that* loud. The last thing we needed was for the police to show up. Oh, the scandal!

Our first night in our new home went amazingly. The next day—not so much. See, we opened gifts. Gretchen gifts. Obviously, nothing represented me, but nothing represented Ant, either. The fact that he'd put up with my sister for so many years amazed me. The man was a saint. A home should represent the *people* who lived inside, not only *one person*.

"I'm sure we can exchange it," he tried to reassure me for like the millionth time when we opened yet another place setting that neither of us would ever use. Beautifully floral Royal Doulton chintz pattern china. Elegant. Fit the feel of the house. It didn't fit the feel of Penelope. Or Ant, for that matter.

"All right, enough of this," Ant ordered. "Did you call Sierra or Gloria yet?"

I cocked my head and gave him my best '*Really?*' eyes. That man knew damn well between sleeping and our nocturnal bedroom activities that had spilled over into the morning, and then eating and opening presents... "Uh, where was I supposed to find the time?"

Per his usual, he laughed at my antics, but said, "Let's try to set it up for Friday. Then we can head to the store."

"*Gasp.*" I threw my hand to my chest. "Are you suggesting, Mr. McCain, that we do a servant's task? Why I never—"

He tackled me onto the sofa, where we wrestled, breaking out into fits of laughter.

"Knock, knock," we heard coming from the front of the house in my mother's distinctly Mrs. Howell pretentiousness. Jessamine must have forgotten to lock the door when she arrived this morning. Our two mothers stepped into the formal living room, where my mother scowled. "Whatever are you doing?"

Ant shrugged, still holding me. "Wrestling," he said. I bit back my laugh.

"Why would you be wrestling my daughter, and around these expensive gifts?"

"Oh, I wasn't wrestling *your* daughter," he insisted. "I was wrestling *my* wife."

"*Stanton*," his mother admonished.

At the same time I offered, "Because we didn't have water guns?" as an excuse, and the both of us fell back onto each other cracking up.

"Helena," my mother called to his mother. "Are they high?"

"Stanton, you aren't *high*, are you?" Helena asked, totally affronted.

I stopped laughing and straightened. "No. Neither of us is high. We were simply having fun. You should try it once in a while."

"*Penelope*." My mother admonished me this time.

"What can we do for you?" Ant asked the mothers.

"We're all having lunch at the club. Helena heard you'd gotten back last night and we thought you should join us."

"Thank you, Mother, Evelyn, but Pen and I have plans today."

"What plans could you possibly have?" my mother asked. Now, our plans included calling our friends and going to the store to buy groceries for a cookout, but they didn't need to know that. Neither of us answered and Ant stared the mothers down until Helena's cheeks pinked.

"Really, son. Do you have to be so crass?" she asked, coming up with her own conclusion as to our plans.

"I just got married," he replied, playing into it.

"And you *just* returned from a month-long honeymoon. You should have gotten that out of your system by now."

"Poor Father," he muttered, causing me to once again bite my bottom lip to keep from laughing.

"Fine." My mother flipped her hand in the air as if dismissing this whole conversation. "You have today to get that out of your system, but tomorrow—"

"Let me cut you off there, Evelyn. Pen and I will be busy until next week. We've got a whole house to set up before I go back to work next Monday."

"What's there to set up? Gretchen already did the work for you."

Leave it to my mother to make such a thoughtless remark, killing my good mood. I slumped in Ant's arms. He shook his head, squeezing me. "Gretchen doesn't live here. Penelope does and she's *not* Gretchen. Now I'm going to have to ask you both to leave, as you've clearly made my wife upset. Oh—and no more unexpected visits. You'll call first. Is that understood?"

"*Stanton*," Helena shouted as my mother threw her hand to her chest.

"Why, I never," Mother hissed. "Stanton McCain, that is not how you speak to your mother-in-law." In my opinion, it was *exactly* what his mother-in-law deserved.

"Please, Mother, Helena," I said, wading in. "That's a sensitive subject for the both of us, as I'm sure you can understand. He's very protective of me because of the judgments we've faced since the wedding was announced. We'd be happy to join you next week, but we ask that you give us this week to put our lives in order."

"We can give them this week," Helena said, and I honestly thought she'd developed a soft spot for me because I stepped in to save the day.

"This week," my mother, who clearly held no such soft spots for me, decreed. "But you *will* show for dinner on Tuesday."

"Tuesday," I said, plastering on that fake smile that I hadn't used since Ant and I had left for Europe.

I knew we should've stayed in Greece.

Chapter Sixteen

Ant threw open the door to Sierra waiting on the stoop for us to answer. Gloria turned into the driveway right after. I opened my arms to hug my friend. She hugged me back as we waited for Glory to reach us. It was a beautiful night for a cookout. Our first in our new home. The mothers hadn't called once since Ant sent them away. It ended up being a glorious first-week home despite all the gift returns and exchanges. But the house was coming together. Something both Ant and I could be proud of, something starting to represent both of us.

"Come on in," Ant offered.

We both stepped back inside with Sierra giving the place a quick glance around. "Swanky," she said. "Why do I think there's a painting party in the near future?"

I shrugged. "It's Gretchen's taste, for sure."

Gloria stepped inside the door. "You look great," she said, giving me a hug, too. "Married life suits you."

"When your husband is Ant," I said proudly.

"I take it he never shouted her name," Sierra asked quietly while we waited for Gloria to make her way back over to us after taking in some of the artwork on the walls, causing my cheeks to blush.

"No."

"What was that?" Ant asked.

"Nothing," I said. "Just girl talk." Then I started walking away. "Come on, ladies. Let me give you a tour."

"So?" Sierra asked when we were far enough away from Ant for him not to hear us.

"So?" I asked back.

"Woman, don't you *so* me. Spill the tea, sister."

"Where should I start? Where he booked us first class for our flight or that he surprised me by paying a boatload of money to change our itinerary?"

"He changed your itinerary? No Paris?"

"No Paris. He surprised me with Cordoba, Spain and we did a tour of the Mediterranean, ending in Crete."

"First class," Gloria sighed.

"You know Philip and Evelyn didn't do flights with the fam. Out of sight, out of mind was always the way we traveled. I'd flown business class plenty, but that was my first time."

My friends *ooh*ed and *ah*ed as I led them to each room, even though we all knew this was the house that Gretchen built.

"I take it that since you're oozing Penelope joy, you got honeymoon nookie?" Gloria asked.

"More in the last month than the last several years of my life," I answered a little giddily.

"He's good?" she asked.

"Girl... you have no idea. It's fun and wild and exciting. I had no idea sex could be like that," I answered as we walked out to the backyard over to the fire pit, where I extended my arm out, offering them seats.

"Telling tales?" Ant asked, surprising me, and I jumped. Sierra, Gloria, and I started laughing like fools.

"Not at all." I walked over to hug him, wrapping my arms around his waist and pressing my face to his chest. He draped his arm around me, holding me back.

"Pen, Sierra, Gloria, you remember my cousin Cormac?"

Oh—his cousin and his wife must have arrived while I'd been showing my girls around. One thing I could say about Cormac McCain, he inherited those attractive McCain genes. Same dark hair as Ant and similar gray eyes, though Ant's brewed like storm clouds when he looked at me. Most people thought they were brothers when first meeting them. And like Ant, he dressed casual in jeans and a button-down with the sleeves turned up. He wore blue to Ant's white.

"Yes," I said, smiling at the man. "It's so good to see you again."

He cut an amused glance at my husband, grinning wide. "This is my wife, Liz," Cormac introduced us. She wore a sweet, tentative smile pretty enough that I just knew when she smiled for real, it brightened up her whole face. She had kind eyes, soft, rounded cheeks, and a mane of thick, golden blonde hair to die for. If I had to sum up Liz going off this first meeting: she was a knockout who didn't know it. I liked that for Cormac.

"Hi, Liz. Clearly, you know I'm Penelope. These are my friends Gloria and Sierra. Thank you so much for coming tonight. This is our first cookout at our home." I stepped from Ant's arms to give her a brief, welcoming hug. "Please, sit. Can I get you drinks? We have beer and hard ciders in the mini-fridge, but we have a pretty stocked liquor cabinet if you'd like something else."

"Cider is good," Liz said.

"Beer for me," Cormac answered.

"Gloria? Sierra?" I asked.

A beer for Sierra and a cider for Gloria.

"Beer, Ant?" I asked.

"Sounds good, sweetheart." He kissed the top of my head as he passed me. "I'll get the fire going."

While he did that, I collected all the bottles from the mini fridge, including a cider for myself, handing them out as our friends got comfortable.

"I have to say, I was surprised to get an invite to a cookout," Cormac said. "Cookouts are so below the McCains."

"We go bowling, too," I said. "You'll find that here especially, Ant and I aren't anything like the McCains." To prove my point, I pointed over to the brick grill with outdoor pizza oven, where we had bourbon BBQ chicken grilling and loaded potato wedges baking.

Once the fire roared in the fire pit, Ant walked over to the grill to check on our chicken. It looked done, so I set my bottle down next to my seat to go in to get the sides.

"Do me a favor," Ant said to Cormac. "Get the chicken on the platter while I help Pen get the rest of the stuff."

His cousin nodded, obliging, and Ant followed me into the kitchen, where instead of helping me gather the sides, he spun me into his arms, backing me up against the edge of the counter. "You better eat hearty because you're expending a lot of energy tonight," he said right before kissing me good and thorough.

"Oh, sorry!" Liz shouted, surprising us. She held her hand like a visor shielding her eyes cast down to the floor. "I thought I'd help."

"No worries," said Ant back, winking at her. "We do that kissing thing from time to time. You'll find that I'm rather fond of my wife."

"Well, Pen, it appears you and I have found the two good McCains in the bunch," she said to me.

She wasn't wrong, but then again, she kind of was, what with Ant's and my history. I shot her a genuine smile, pointing to the refrigerator. "You want to bring the chopped salad out?"

Liz nodded, walking over to get the chopped salad, which had corn, black beans, black olives, and fried tortilla strips along with the lettuce, tomato, cucumber, carrot, and shredded sharp cheddar cheese, lightly dressed in a southwest ranch dressing. So *not* typical McCain dinner party fare.

I handed off the plates and flatware to Ant. We used paper plates, albeit thick and expensive paper plates, but paper nonetheless. Our flatware looked like metal but was—*gasp!*—plastic. Elegantly relaxed. That was how Ant described his vision of our cookout at the store. I walked to the refrigerator to grab the tray of condiments for the wedges. Sour cream, spicy jalapeño dip, black olives, chives, sautéed onions, and more of that gloriously thick, spicy BBQ sauce that we coated the chicken with. Before making my way back outside, I grabbed the basket of cornbread muffins.

We ate, talked, and laughed throughout the night. Even eating those gooey s'mores for dessert.

If that weekend ended our honeymoon, then Ant and I went out with a bang. A big, beautiful bang.

Unfortunately, Monday morning came way too soon for my liking. Ant said I didn't have to get up with him, but I wanted to. It gave us time to talk while he got ready for work. I cooked us breakfast and we enjoyed the break, eating and sipping coffee until he had to run.

"I'm calling about converting that extra garage today," he said, "and I'm going to start making preparations to work from home a few days a week."

"You are amazing, Stanton McCain." I pushed up on my toes to kiss him.

Ant looked at me, stroking my cheek with the backs of his fingers. "I keep telling you it's because you're so amazing that I have to keep up." He looked down at his watch. "Do we have time to—"

"Go." I swatted his butt.

He laughed as he kissed me once more before leaving out the door off the kitchen that led to the attached garage. So far, this marriage business had been working out in my favor. After he left, I walked back upstairs to shower and dress for the day. I had no idea where the day would take me, but I one hundred percent expected it to involve Evelyn von Dutton in some capacity.

Oh, how I wished I were wrong. Right as Jessamine, our housekeeper, showed up for work, so too did my mother. "Hey, Jessamine," I greeted the woman. "Get the kids off to school okay?" I adored Jessamine. She was pleasant to talk to, and efficient. It was unfortunate timing that my mother showed now for so many reasons. Jessamine's uniform, for instance. I let the person wearing said uniform pick what they thought would be the most comfortable to work in. In this case, a light blue polo and straight-legged khakis. The light blue of the polo worked nicely with Jessamine's black hair and tan skin tone. It made sense to me. The fact that Jessamine lived in her own place. The fact that I wanted a friendly rapport with a woman who spent a large part of her day in my house. None of these were acceptable in Evelyn von Dutton's world.

"Yes, Mrs. McCain. Thank you for asking."

"Please, Jessamine, I've told you it's Pen. Mrs. McCain is my mother-in-law."

Jessamine snickered, as did I and I hoped this meant that we were done with the whole "Mrs. McCain" thing.

"Really, Penelope. You need to hire some live-in staff and they *never* address you by your name." My mother shoved past me and Jessamine, to stand inside the foyer. "This is unacceptable." She gestured around my home as if it looked like a wild frat party had taken place the night before. We weren't living in *Animal House*. Our home looked lived-in because we lived here, but Ant and I had picked up after the cookout on Friday. Together we'd put the food away and done the dishes. There was this amazing machine called a dishwasher—it was right there in the name! Its sole purpose was to *wash dishes*. Jessamine was hired to vacuum, mop, clean the bathrooms, make the beds, do the laundry, and any of those types of tasks. We shopped out yard work.

I rubbed my hand along my forehead trying to tamp down my irritation and sighed. When that didn't work, I sighed again. Nope, not any better. Having not dealt with my mother for over a month, I lost my touch, letting her get to me. Tequila, I needed tequila—*no I didn't*. I needed to grow a pair and let her know my house, my rules in no uncertain terms. I liked to cook and since I only had to cook for Ant and myself with the exception of a friendly cookout, I saw no reason to hire a chef, which was another thing my mother admonished me for.

Right. You can do this, Pen. I squared my shoulders ready to tell my mother exactly what was what when she got to me first.

"There is no way for you to plan a successful dinner party and cook the food as well." She opened a leather-bound folder that she held, handing me a piece of paper. "Here is a list of the acceptable companies to hire from. All the applicants are vetted, having gone through rigorous background checks. You'll thank me, dear. This list is gold."

Hmm... I totally deflated. "Can I get you some coffee, Mother?" I asked. Point to Evelyn.

She outright frowned at me. "If you had more than one employee, you wouldn't need to fetch me a coffee personally. You'd have someone do it for you. I know I've taught you better."

"Ant and I want our home to be more low-key."

"Ant wants what you tell him he wants. And don't confuse low-key with low class, Penelope. It's very unbecoming for both the Von Duttons and McCains. Of which you are now both."

"You don't have to tell me my name, Mother. I'm very aware of who I married."

"So then you'll start calling right away." Then she handed me another list. "You'll need a personal assistant. Heloise Norton's granddaughter, you know the chubby one? She's just graduated from Princeton, and heaven knows she has no prospects for a husband the way she looks. Working as your assistant would give her some good, real-world experience, because really, what firm would hire a plain, plump girl like her?

"Now, because you haven't yet, I had Stanton's secretary sync your calendar with Stanton's so that you are made aware of any event that arises. Men can be dreadfully behind with mentioning important details like that."

From there, I was swept away for lunch at the club and an afternoon of committee meetings for committees that I didn't sit on.

By the time I got home, I was ready to run away and join the circus. Ant found me in the kitchen mutilating a carrot. He gingerly reached his hand over to grab the handle of the chef's knife, stilling my hand.

"Whoa! Let me just take that, sweetheart." He set his briefcase down on the countertop along with the knife and turned me into his arms. "What happened?"

"We have a staff now," I cried, like with actual tears.

"*What?*" he laughed.

"A staff. Some of them are going to live here. They'll sleep in the third-floor servants' quarters. And I have a personal assistant, and I'm synced to your calendar. And I sat in on meeting after meeting of committees I'm not even a part of. It all happened without my control. She's an unstoppable force, Ant. I tried to stand up to her, but you've seen Evelyn von Dutton in action. So now, if you'll kindly hand me my knife, I'll finish dinner." More tears fell. I wiped at my eyes with my shoulder waiting with my hand out for the knife back.

"Nope." He grabbed my hand, walking me into the den, where he deposited me down on the sofa. "Pizza?" he asked.

"But I'm supposed to—"

He used his magic lips to silence me. "Sweetheart, you've had a day. Let's veg out in front of the TV for the rest of the night. Then, I'll do that thing you like..." He trailed off, waggling his eyebrows suggestively, and I smiled for the first time in hours.

"Okay. Mushroom and green olive?" I asked, hopeful.

"Is there any other kind?"

"I mean... depends on my mood."

He pulled me onto his lap, straddling him, to hug me. "I'm going up to change. I'll call our order in on my way."

"Thanks for being so wonderful, Ant."

"I should've realized how your day would go and been prepared for it. All I got were back pats from colleagues glad to have me back and getting cornered by the dirty old men of the lot who wanted play-by-plays of our honeymoon."

Looking at the floor demurely, I cracked a smile. "Did you tell them?"

"Oh, yeah—I told them all about how my new wife is a shriveled-up old prune who only believes in sex for procreation."

"Well, as long as you showed me in a positive light."

He got me with another hot lip maneuver and I was half-undressed by the time he remembered the food, pulling away, mumbling, "*Pizza*—dammit."

Everything he did made me fall deeper in love with him. Even if he never loved me back, I couldn't complain. Most women who got to choose their husbands didn't have it as good as me.

I just hoped he felt the same way.

Fingers crossed.

Chapter Seventeen

The chimes sounded from the doorbell on the front door to Gerald and Helena's massive Greek Revival house. It screamed money, including everything that made it Greek. Pilasters, columns, a porch entry, a window in the pediment, and plain or highly decorated cornices and friezes. As we'd just spent a week in Greece, I felt confident in saying that my in-laws basically lived in the Acropolis—though, yes, the Acropolis wasn't a house. I got that. Get over it.

They might have been his parents, but neither of our families gave off that *"this will always be your home"* vibe. Thus, we waited to be let in. The longer we stood outside, the more I appreciated the life Ant and I were building together. Our children, should we have any, would grow up knowing that no matter where they went in the world, they always had a place to come back to.

Imelda, one of their housekeepers, answered the door, which meant Douglas, the butler, must have been busy.

"Mr. Stanton," she greeted. Imelda came to the McCains from San Diego, after settling there from the Philippines. A fact I knew very well because the Philippines was yet another place I wanted to travel to. And with Ant by my side, I bet I would. Her sister Fernanda already worked for the family. Imelda loved Ant.

Her eyes twinkled whenever she saw him, and she smiled broadly. "And your bride, Ms. Penelope." She moved out of our way. "Please, come in."

"Thank you, Imelda," he answered. "It's good to see you. Are the Von Duttons here yet?"

"Yes. They're already in the parlor having drinks."

Ant took my hand, leading me to the parlor. My nerves started getting the better of me. I had no idea why. These people, whether I liked it or not, were family. But it felt like once we stepped inside that room, the expectations for Stanton and Penelope would completely disintegrate the reality of Ant and Pen.

"Stanton." Gerald greeted us. "Glad you're here, son." He walked over to where we stood just inside to pat Ant on the back with several back slaps. "Penelope... you look lovely, as always. My wife says you enjoyed your time in Paris."

"We didn't go to Paris. Ant—*erm*—Stanton surprised me with a trip along the Mediterranean. Italy and Greece were my favorites, but the whole trip..." I cut a glance to Ant, getting choked up from the memories of how we'd started off our married lives. "It was better than I dreamed it would be."

My husband dropped my hand to wrap his arms around me from behind. "Douglas," Gerald called. The large man in his dark suit appeared in the doorway, waiting. "Get Stanton and Penelope here their drinks, please."

"Certainly." He nodded at Gerald. "What can I get you?"

"A Manhattan for Pen and Tom Collins for me, if you don't mind."

"Not a problem at all, sir," he said before turning out of the room.

Before Douglas got back with our drinks, Imelda showed up to the room with two more people in tow. Ant moved us toward a settee as she announced, "The Hendersons."

The Hendersons? No one said this was an actual dinner party. Mr. Henderson was the County Commissioner. He reminded me of an English Bulldog, only, an English Bulldog with a bulbous nose. His wife fit right in with Evelyn and Helena, stick thin and nipped and tucked on every portion of her body that was nipable and tuckable.

Thank goodness both Ant and I knew better than to dress comfortably when dining with either of our families. Ant wore a suit similar to what he'd worn to work today. This one navy-blue silk with a monochrome shirt and tie of ice blue while I wore a slim-fitting plum-colored dress that buttoned all the way down the front. Vintage. From 1940. With shoulder pads and the hem fell to mid-shin. I loved this dress. Given the way we'd almost missed dinner with the family when he walked into the bedroom and saw me wearing it, Ant loved this dress, too. It was nothing that my sister would have ever put on her body. I didn't know, nor did I want to know, if he ever had that kind of reaction to something she'd worn, but knowing he found me that attractive, well, let's just say it was good for my ego.

Douglas came back with our drinks and he left again to fetch the drinks for the Hendersons. While the conversation went on around us, Ant leaned in to whisper in my ear, "Sweetheart, you can't wear that perfume to dinner parties anymore. I'm in my parents' home, but all I want to do is fuck my wife again."

I laughed, my sigh both turned on and uncomfortable. "We can always make our excuses early."

"Don't think we won't." He nipped at my earlobe. Nipped at it. In his parents' house.

Thankfully, Douglas used that moment to deliver the Hendersons' drinks and announce, "Dinner is ready. Please, if you'd make your way to the dining room."

We let the room empty out before we followed with our drink glasses in hand. Ant pulled out my seat for me before he sat next to me.

"So you enjoyed your honeymoon?" Mr. Henderson asked Ant.

"Very much," he replied.

Mr. Henderson eyed me up and down in a way that made me feel icky. "Well," he said. "She is a pretty little thing."

My husband reached his hand under the table to give my knee a squeeze. "That, she is."

I smiled at him, taking a sip of my Manhattan.

"Can we expect a baby announcement soon?" Mr. Henderson asked, causing me to choke on my drink, coughing. Ant patted my back.

Who asked that?

Why did rich men think it was okay to ask such personal questions? When was the last time you had unprotected sex, Mr. Henderson?

"No," Ant answered for the both of us. "We'd like to take some time for just us before we decide to bring children into the mix." One of the kitchen servers, Lance, rolled a cart in carrying the soup course. He set a bowl down in front of Mrs. Henderson and worked his way around the table, ending with Gerald.

Carrot. I loved carrot soup.

"You're going to want to go with sooner rather than later, son," Mr. Henderson said back. I hated the condescending way rich men called younger men "son." *Ant's not your son, my dude.*

"And why is that?" Ant asked and I could feel him tense next to me.

"Voters prefer traditional families with traditional values."

"Voters?" I asked as I felt the few spoonfuls of soup begin to turn in my stomach.

"Terry Eliot is stepping down from the city council due to health reasons. They're holding a special election in a couple of months," Gerald said, joining in. "This is the perfect opportunity for you to get in there."

Ant frowned at his father. "I have no interest in running for city council. Between that and my job, I'd never see Pen. We're newlyweds. I'd like to spend time with her."

"Gerald," Mr. Henderson said. "Talk some sense into the

boy." He threw his hand out toward me. "You can wake her up to fuck just as easily as doing it before she sleeps."

My face began to burn with humiliation.

"*Jesus, Thomas,*" Ant bit out. "She's my wife, not a sex doll."

"What do you think the wedding was for?" My dad asked and my mouth dropped open. I'd been pimped out by my father?

"The wedding was to turn your daughter into my personal sex toy?" he asked, clearly astonished.

"The wedding—" He pointed his narrowed gaze at my husband. "was to give you a traditional family and keep you from getting caught up in any scandals."

"I wasn't involved in any scandals before the wedding."

"Grow up, Stanton," Gerald barked at his son. "If you think the people who knew about Gretchen weren't talking, you're delusional."

"And whose fault was that, Father?"

"I'm not the one who couldn't keep his girlfriend happy."

"*Gerald—*" Helena cried.

"That's not how it works!" I exploded. Why? I should have just let the others in the room hash this out, but no—Ant and I were in this together. They had no right to go after him, even if it brought their wrath onto my shoulders, too. "She left Ant for Gabby. There wasn't anything else Ant could've done. None of you ever bothered to ask her if she was even attracted to men."

Whoa! That was the wrong thing to say. The anger and disgust that stared back at me from around the table would have cowed me without Ant by my side. I didn't do confrontation well. One might call it a defining feature of my life, avoiding confrontation by deflection with sarcasm and humor. In other words, I preferred to live an *avoid-it-at-all-costs* lifestyle.

"And don't think we don't regret that we now have to work around that," Thomas, Mr. Henderson, said ruefully. "Tell us, Penelope, any flings with women we need to be aware of? Sex clubs? Orgies? We'd hate to be blindsided by any skeletons in your closet."

Ant pushed up from his chair, grabbing my hand and pulling me up with him. "Do not *ever* talk to my wife like that again." He started walking and if I didn't quicken my steps, I'd have stumbled behind him. "Come on, Pen. We're going."

Helena shot up from her seat. "Stanton, please. Gerald, stop them."

"I'm sorry, Mother," Ant said. "We'll have *you* over for dinner soon."

He kept a firm grip on my hand, picking up the pace the closer to the front door we walked. And it wasn't until we got outside that I finally got him to stop. "Ant, *please.*"

He stopped abruptly, and he turned to me, his face lined with tension. "I didn't marry you to have someone to fuck without a scandal."

I pressed my hands to his chest. "I know that," I said gently. "You've never been anything but good to me, Ant. Please don't let them ruin your night."

"Too late for that."

"Do you want to go for a drive?"

"Pen, how can you be so calm? Our parents just admitted that they pimped you out to me. And Thomas Henderson—that man's lucky he didn't end up with a black eye."

"He's nothing to us, Ant."

He sighed and the tension left his body, replaced by resignation, maybe, as his arms slid around me and he leaned his forehead against mine. "You jumped in when you didn't have to—drew the fire away from me."

"We're in this together, Ant. It was a bit of a shock hearing my dad talk like that, but I'm not stupid. I knew they wanted our families joined for a reason. But you—you've always been one of my best friends. That hasn't changed because we spoke some vows and bumped uglies. Those things solidify my loyalty to you, Stanton McCain. Totally and completely."

He moved his hands to my face, pressing his lips to mine, and I opened to him, body, mind, and soul. He kissed me on his parents' front lawn like he wanted to climb inside me. "What did I do to deserve you?" he asked, though I didn't think he really expected an answer.

I shook my head, unable to answer even if he did.

"Come on." Ant grabbed my hand again, pulling me toward the Jag behind him. He stopped us to open my door. Again. Thinking about it, Ant *always* opened my door. I realized just now that it started way back when we were kids, but he'd been upping his door opening since our engagement. I slid onto the seat, clicking my seatbelt as he shut my door. It might seem like a little thing to most people, but to me, that was the act of a true friend. If he wanted to know why I put myself in the line of fire for him, there you go. He opened my door. He remembered I drank Manhattans. He appreciated my love of all things vintage. The list just went on and on. Now was my time to reciprocate— to be a true friend back to him.

Ant and Pen, taking on the world together.

After he buckled himself in, he turned in the direction of the lake. The big one, as in Huron, and we drove.

For over an hour, we took in the water and the twinkling stars.

"They aren't going to let this go, you know?" he said finally.

"*I know.*" And I did. I totally knew they were going to beat this horse relentlessly.

"Pen, I don't even believe in their politics. Traditional families with traditional values? Do '*traditional families*' have children for trophies? Does '*traditional values*' include pimping out your kids to further *your* political aspirations? I don't want any part of it."

Being the wife of a city councilman didn't wet my panties, either. We had plans. Ant working from home. Me working in my own studio. Traveling together. Getting comfortable in the life we were building together. And when we finally did have kids...

"Then don't," I said.

"What?"

"If you don't want to, then *don't*. We owe them nothing. This is our life. They had their chances. Neither your father nor mine ran for office. It's not our fault if they didn't take advantage of it. What is a traditional family, anyway? You've never said you even want to have kids with me—"

"Of course I want kids," he said.

"But with me?"

"Pen, I have one wife and you're it. When I plant babies in a woman, she's you. But I can't deny that I'd like us to have time to just be a couple for a while first."

"I want that, too."

"Great," he said, the tension leaving the car, and I glanced over in time to see the smirk spread across his lips. "Now that we've got that part hashed out, I didn't get the chance to tell you yet, but I'm working from home tomorrow because the contractor is showing to check out the extra garage for the studio."

As we agreed on our big *FU* to our parents, it hit me that Philip and Evelyn, and Gerald and Helena made a huge mistake shoving us together.

And I laughed.

Chapter Eighteen

Giddy excitement bubbled up inside me as Ant led me into our bathroom. He turned on the faucet in the giant clawfoot tub, holding his hand under the cascade to check for temperature. We'd showered together before to get clean and have sex, but we'd never soaked in the tub to reconnect and chill.

He began by unbuttoning my dress while I stepped out of my heels. He slid the garment off my shoulders, tossing it onto the hamper against the subway-tiled wall and immediately gliding his hand over my bared skin to catch the spaghetti strap and rid me of my slip. When he turned to toss that onto my dress, I unhooked my bra. His eyes heated when faced with my breasts, but he didn't press the advantage by touching my body in any sensual way or bending in to kiss me. He ran his hands along my curves to snag my panties, dragging them down my legs, and he waited as I stepped out of them. He tossed those onto the growing pile on the hamper, too.

"Get in," he ordered softly while taking my hand to help me into the water. I sighed all the sighs as the warm wetness caressed my skin. As I got comfortable, my husband left the bathroom. He was gone for several minutes, only to show up again with two glasses of pink moscato in hand.

After taking a sip of his, he handed both glasses off to me to begin stripping down. I watched intently as he disrobed. I knew what it felt like to run my fingers through that chest hair, to dance them over the skin on his abs and the glory that happy trail of thick hair below the navel led to.

The longer I stared at it, the more his member twitched under my perusal, but he didn't make any moves to start things up. Once fully naked, he climbed in behind me and sat. The water level rose to cover my breasts and he used his toes to turn off the faucet while lifting his glass from my hand. I leaned back against his chest, getting comfortable again.

"We didn't get to eat dinner," he said, pressing a kiss to the hair above my ear then taking a sip of his wine. "I ordered us Italian. They said it'll be about an hour. I figure the water will be cold by then."

"You're such a considerate husband." I sipped my wine.

"I try. Cormac called while I was getting the wine."

"You were busy. Calling in food and talking to your cousin. I'm impressed. You weren't gone that long."

"I had incentive to get back up here." He sipped on more of his wine. "Anyway, he and Liz want us to go out to dinner with them Friday."

"What did you tell him?"

"I said what any husband should say. 'Let me check with my wife and I'll get back to you.'"

"Good answer."

"Well, you know... I'm learning."

"What do you think we'd be doing right now if we weren't Von Dutton McCains?"

"Am I still married to you in this scenario?"

I shrugged. "Sure."

"Then I'd be right here in the tub with my wife. It might be a much smaller tub and we'd be drinking far cheaper wine, but I can't think of any husband who'd want to be anywhere but naked with a woman as beautiful as you, Pen. What about you?"

"Well, I'd probably be working some entry-level position that royally ticked me off because all I really want to do is make art. We'd probably be living in an apartment rather than this huge house."

"You're a screamer, sweetheart. I don't think we'd live in an apartment for too long. Our neighbors would get jealous."

Holy crap! I couldn't believe he just said that. "*Ant.*"

"*What?*" His laugh held a hint of mischief. "You clearly aren't paying attention to your climax."

"Oh, I'm paying attention, big guy."

"'Big guy,' eh?" He plucked my glass from my hand to set it on the table next to the bath, then set his down next to mine and he lifted me up to spin me. I leaned to the right to avoid the faucet as Ant cradled my left foot in his hand, pressing his thumbs into the arch, rubbing it.

"Oh, oh, *oh*... Stanton McCain... this would be the time to ask anything of me."

"Really?" he asked, setting my left foot back into the water on his lap and picking up the right to give it the same attention.

"Your wish is my command."

He set my foot back down into the water, taking my hand to pull me up. I straddled his lap as I bent in to kiss him. I smiled against his mouth as his tongue stroked into mine and he lifted me to take him. I rode him unhurried. My husband was an amazing orgasm giver.

"Of anything you could have asked for," I started on a down glide, "bathtub sex is what you chose?"

"What can I say? I don't need much more than this."

The sweetest orgasm in the world hit right before the doorbell rang. He took a moment to collect himself before lifting me off his lap. Ant pecked my nose then climbed out. He wrapped a towel around his waist and then bent over to fish his wallet out of his pants.

"Meet you in bed." He winked.

It took me a bit longer than it took him to be able to stand and climb out of the tub. I tugged the towel off the towel bar, wrapping it around myself under my arms, and pulled the stopper. Then I walked back into the bedroom to throw something on. I chose one of Ant's white V-neck T-shirts because with the thin cotton, the fabric was rather see-through, so it said sexy without trying to be sexy.

He walked into the room as I was setting our wine glasses on each of our bedside tables. "You answered the door in your towel?" I asked and bit my lip, shaking my head at his utter lack of decorum.

"I didn't want to keep the kid waiting."

"I'm sure the kid didn't mind."

"Well he did ask me out for Friday, but I told him I already had plans."

"You're an idiot." I laughed as I patted the bed. "Now how about you feed me?"

I loved getting to see his playful side. How could I have *not* fallen in love with Ant all those years ago when this was how he acted? Only now it was so much better because I got the sexy times as well. He dropped the bags onto the bed and set down the bottle of wine before fishing a pair of cotton shorts out of his drawer.

The bags were filled with foil containers. I peeled the cardboard topper off each as I pulled it from the bag. Fettuccine Alfredo. Linguini with clam sauce, chicken piccata, a salad, and fluffy breadsticks.

"You spoil me," I said while taking one of the thick paper plates left over from the cookout that he brought upstairs for us.

"This?" he said as he started pulling the dishes closer to him. "This is mine. I figured you could make yourself a peanut butter and jelly."

Oh, no, he did not. I reached over the food, giving him a good old-fashioned nipple twist. He howled but laughed at the same time. "*Okay*... there's probably enough to share."

Nothing *probably* about it. "Don't ever get between a Penelope and her Italian food."

"Noted," he said, handing me off a fork, then he picked up the remote and turned on the television hanging on the wall opposite the bed.

We spent the evening watching National Geographic and eating delicious Italian food that was *almost* as good as the food we'd eaten in Italy. Somehow, he turned it into a really great night.

The next day, Ant moved between working in his office and collaborating with me and the contractor to come up with the best studio for me to work in. I really disliked the contractor. He looked maybe ten years older than me but talked *at* me, not *to* me, like I was a *four-year-old*.

"I'm only here as a second set of ears," he told the man, who spent most of the time trying to get Ant's opinion on everything despite Ant telling the man several times, "She's the boss on this project."

I could've kissed Ant and I was about a second and a half away from turning the contractor into a eunuch by the time the man left. But he'd come to us highly recommended. So I supposed I could put up with him for the end result that Ant and I both envisioned.

It was also move-in day for the new staff. I hated the thought of strangers living in my house. Again, they came highly recommended from the list my mother had given me, but if my husband and I were going to do our own thing, did we really need them?

We definitely needed to chat about that once we were alone.

Since we'd already employed Jessamine, I put her in charge of the other housekeepers to relegate duties to be done and I bumped her up in pay to compensate for taking on a leadership role.

One of the new girls, Lissa, listened to Jessamine when she gave an order and made some excellent coffee. Still, that wasn't enough of a reason to retain a staff if we didn't need one. She was a tiny thing, although, I could tell she was a hard worker. I was so confused.

My mother called a couple of different times and I let each one go to voicemail. She'd be lucky if I ever talked to her or my father again.

Wednesday night, Ant and I went over to Sierra's house for game night. Gloria showed as well as some of Sierra's work friends.

She pulled out *Redneck Life*, which was exactly what it sounded like. The game of *Life* but in a redneck edition. On my first turn, I found out that I'd completed the fifth grade and ended up as a monster truck rally announcer as my career.

Gloria graduated high school and ran a successful mullet salon. It went on from there. Ant got married, divorced, remarried, and had a houseful of kids. I only had two.

"You get the kid question yet?" Sierra asked me and I looked down at my cards.

"Yeah—two."

"No. I mean in real life. With you two back from the honeymoon."

I rolled my eyes, looking to my husband. "Did you hear that, Ant? Did we get the kid question?"

He popped a handful of caramel corn into his mouth, chewed, swallowed, then broke it down for her. "Henderson, the County Clerk, was at dinner last night. That jackass had the nerve to ask if I'd knocked Pen up yet."

The game sort of stopped from there. "You're kidding?" Gloria asked.

"Wish I were. Like, he barely knows Pen and me, but he's asking about our sex life? How disgusting is that?"

"Very," Sierra's coworker friend Crystal answered. She wore her hair dyed silver and had a hoop through her nose. And she wore these thick, pink-framed cat eyeglasses. She was so cute.

And wasn't that just the understatement of the week—about Henderson being disgusting, not about Crystal being cute.

"The whole dinner went downhill and turned really ugly," Ant went on. "I wanted to eviscerate every man at that table. If Pen hadn't been there, I might have. But I didn't want to spend the first years of our marriage in prison. Most no longer do conjugal visits."

I threw a handful of popcorn at him. "I'm getting another beer," I said, pushing up from my seat, and walked into the kitchen. Sierra followed me in.

"How'd it 'turn ugly'?" she asked.

"They told Ant that I needed to pop a kid out because they wanted him to run for office and voters preferred *'traditional families with traditional values.'*"

Her mouth fell open.

"Yeah. It gets worse. Ant said he didn't want to run for office and my own father was like, '*What do you think the wedding was for?*'"

"*What?*"

"Oh yeah—then they brought up Gretch and Gerald was all '*I'm not the one who couldn't keep my girlfriend happy.*'"

"You can't be serious." She handed me a couple of beers to carry, while she took the rest.

"I totally am. Being married to Ant has been the best thing for me, but the worst for him because no matter how hard we try to be different from our families, they keep digging their claws in. I hate that they're making me feel bad for Gretchen."

"Oh, my God! I am right there with you. She disliked me, couldn't stand Gloria, and was up her own butt half the time."

I gave a half-hearted laugh. "*Half* the time?"

Her laugh wasn't half-hearted, and then neither was mine. "And he doesn't seem to be complaining," she said.

"That's only because of the sex. We're kind of explosive between the sheets. If we didn't have that..." Hearing myself say that out loud hurt. I wanted him to love me, to need me in his life the way I loved and needed him.

"*Pen*." She rested a hand against my arm. "No matter the reason he's there, he's there and he's loyal to you."

I smiled at her. "You're right. I'm just being a whiner."

"Did you say a *wiener*?"

"Who's a wiener?" the man himself asked, surprising the both of us after popping into the kitchen.

"This guy from my honeymoon," I answered, shooting him a wink.

"*Is* one or *has* a big one?"

Sierra shook her head and I patted his chest as we passed him. "You keep dreaming there, fella."

He pulled me back to him, his voice dripping with innuendo, low and full of promise. "Oh, you're in so much trouble when we get home, sweetheart." Then he nipped my ear and I couldn't wait to get home.

Chapter Nineteen

"Pen, you almost done?" Ant called to me up the stairs while I stood in front of the mirror in my master bath with the door open, checking my makeup one last time and hooking in my second earring.

"Coming," I yelled back, stumbling into the room to slide on my heels and grab up my clutch before running down the stairs.

"Whoa! I'd rather be late than have you break your neck, sweetheart."

"You get fast or safe, McCain." I placed my hand on his chest once I reached the last step, pressing a kiss to his smiling lips.

He dropped his hand to my back, moving us to the garage. Once we were both buckled in, he pressed the button on the remote door opener, started the car, and backed out. We were on our way into the city tonight, heading to a restaurant in downtown Detroit to meet Cormac and Liz for dinner.

"If I haven't told you yet, you look amazing, Pen."

I reached over the center console to pat his thigh. "Thanks."

Ant captured my hand, keeping it in place. "I'm serious. You just keep upping your glamor game."

"Well, you're pretty hot yourself."

"I want you to know—" Whatever he was about to say got cut

off when a dark SUV ran a red light. Ant slammed his hand on the horn, wrenching the steering wheel while stomping on the brake. The Jag skidded. The tires squealed. My heart hammered in my chest.

"Oh my god!" I had my hand pressed to my heart. "I think that just took ten years off my life."

"You okay?"

"I'm fine, though I might have peed myself a little. Are you okay?"

"I'm good. I just—shit, that was close."

"Well, he's long gone. Let's not let it ruin the rest of our night."

Part of him must have agreed with me because he moved my hand back to his thigh as he righted the car and continued through the intersection, but he kept both hands on the wheel from that point on.

Good thing it took us time to get to Detroit or I highly doubted I'd have been able to eat a thing. It took forever for my stomach to settle. Ant found a parking lot close to the restaurant. We paid, parked, and then hoofed it. Downtown Detroit looked amazing. The lights. The buzz of excitement that seemed to effervesce from the people having fun.

He opened the door of the restaurant, allowing me to walk inside first. Low light. A modern take on upscale dining utilizing straight-lined wooden furniture but pairing it with gas fireplaces surrounded by cement hearths.

We stopped at the hostess's desk. "We're joining the McCain party," Ant said and the chick, who gave off an *'I know I'm hot"* vibe, admired my husband a little too long for my liking before she looked down at the screen to find their table. I mean, she definitely was hot and it took a lot of confidence to give bedroom eyes to another woman's husband right in front of said woman—especially when she was wearing a uniform of a black button-down and black slacks when I wore an actual, *modern* LBD just for this occasion. I bit my lip to keep from telling her "eyes on your own paper." I didn't want to embarrass Ant.

She led us to a table in the back corner of the room, where Cormac and Liz were already seated, drinks in hand.

"Stanton," Cormac said when he saw us, standing to shake Ant's hand. "Penelope." He greeted me next, giving me a cheek kiss, then gestured for us to sit, which we did after giving Liz her cheek kisses.

"Thanks for inviting us," I said, sipping on the glass of ice water that already sat at my place setting. "We almost showed up as ghosts."

He knitted his eyebrows in question. "What?"

"Some asshole ran a red," Ant answered for me. "And all I'm saying is thank God, it's clear, dry, and warm out. If it had been winter, we'd have definitely missed dinner."

"Shit, man, you all right?"

"We're both fine. Just a little shaken." Ant picked up his water, taking a sip.

"Well, I, for one, am glad you didn't die,' Liz said. As we nodded she finished, "You're the only ones from Corm's family that I like." At that, she and I began giggling. I couldn't stop. Humor and sarcasm. She fit in just fine. Liz needed to join us for our next girls' night.

The server showed up to take our drink orders. Ant and I ordered champagne because it seemed like a champagne kind of night.

Cormac put his elbows on the table and folded his hands, a serious look on his face. "So my brother called me the other night and he said he heard from my dad that you're dipping your toes into politics, and I thought, Stanton? It's your right and I'm not trying to talk you out of your politics, but I've been pretty vocal about where I stand. I wanted us to have dinner because I loved the BBQ at your house, but now I have to know if this is going to put a ripple in our relationship. You and my brother are the only family I see since Liz and I married. Am I losing you, too, buddy?"

Ant laughed sarcastically. "You're *not* losing me. We had a disastrous dinner on Tuesday night where they told me I was running for office and I told them what they could do with that order."

"Tuesday night? I talked to my brother on Wednesday. My dad found out at lunch on Wednesday from Uncle Gerald."

"Shit." Ant wiped his hand over his face. "You've got to be kidding me."

"I wish I were."

"Not happening. You would've been disgusted if you'd heard the shit they said about Pen, me, our marriage. I'm still fuming."

"We have a fair idea," Liz said. "We got our share of vitriol when Corm told them we were getting married. 'You want to fuck low class, have at it. You don't parade them around dignitaries.'"

"Still so sorry about that, baby," Cormac said to his wife, pressing his forehead to her hair.

Ant looked ready to kill someone, and I couldn't blame him. "I'm not doing it. And if I ever do, they will live to regret every nasty thing they've said or done to everyone *not* them—but especially our women."

"Okay, enough of the heavy," I said, laying my hand down on his arm in solidarity. "Let's look at the menu." When Ant nodded, I smiled, finishing, "At least you're prepared."

"You make everything better, Pen," Ant said before leaning in to kiss my cheek.

My darling dinner companions weren't at all embarrassed when I ordered the personal chanterelle mushroom with arugula and goat cheese pizza. Nor were they bothered when Ant ordered the espresso-crusted beef tenderloin with crispy, smashed red potatoes and we shared. In a fancy restaurant.

They did the same, but with different dishes. It made me sad to think that my parents had never shared a meal in a restaurant, or even worse, they used to but stopped because it didn't look right. So no, the pizza wasn't exactly drippy, but come on, *pizza*.

The beef tasted particularly rich and well, beefy, as well.

For dessert, just like with dinner, we shared strawberry mousse, along with a fresh strawberry-topped pavlova, and a chocolate pots de crème.

"I don't think I'll eat again for a week," I said as I licked the last bit of chocolate off my spoon.

"Me, either." Liz pushed her plate away. "So Corm and I were thinking about going to Europe after the holidays, but we're not sure where to go. He's been. I never have. What was your favorite place?"

"That's hard. Venice was amazing, but Crete—" Ant looked at me, then back at his cousins.

"Crete," we both said at the same time.

"I know Ant said you head up to your folks' place for Christmas," I said. "I haven't talked to my hubby about this yet, but I was thinking it would be nice to do a Friendsgiving this year."

"That's an amazing idea, sweetheart." He kissed my cheek. "Only a couple of months away. It'd be good to get the RSVPs so we don't find ourselves alone with service for twelve."

Cormac turned to his wife and they whispered between them. "Even if it's just the four of us, that would be great. Liz's parents always head out to California to be with her mom's sister for Thanksgiving. Jimmy and Grace go to their in-laws." Jimmy and Grace were, I deduced, and then had it confirmed, Liz's brother and sister. Then, Cormac looked Ant right in the eyes and said, "I'm so damn glad you married Pen instead of Gretchen."

"What my husband means," Liz said, cutting in, "is that we liked Gretchen, but she tended to follow your family guidelines and you know the families wouldn't approve of us having dinner together tonight, let alone a holiday."

They weren't wrong. Gretchen, she followed my parents' directives to a T—well, until she'd run off with her secret girlfriend to get married. Semantics.

"*I'm* glad I married Pen instead of Gretchen. No need to

sugarcoat it on our account, Liz. I still don't know how I got so lucky."

Ending on that high note, Ant paid our bill and we left them by their car to walk around the downtown, taking in the nightlife. The casino was hopping as always and Comerica had a concert going on.

"If I'd known we'd be doing all this walking, I wouldn't have worn these heels." I mean, we as women sacrificed a lot for a sexy pair of heels that made our legs look amazing, comfort being one of the biggest. Still... "I think you're going to have to carry me to the car."

And before I knew what was happening, Ant swept me up into his arms, carrying me bride-style back to the car. I wrapped my arms around his neck and hung on for dear life even as I laughed like there was no tomorrow.

He unlocked the Jag and set me in the front seat, then opened up the back door to retrieve something. He brought out my favorite pair of leather flip-flops. I gasped, shooting up from the seat to hug him, peppering his face with kisses. "Oh my god! I love you, Ant." Yeah, those words slipped out. "For doing this," I tried to cover. "Thank you."

Things got real weird between us after I let fly. We didn't really talk on the way home, but I noticed him cutting secret glances at me and I couldn't help but wonder if I'd just crossed an uncrossable line.

Stupid, stupid, Pen. How could I have told him that? We had sex and friendship. Those were what we were working with. I felt my eyes begin to brim with tears that—*mayday, mayday*—were starting to fall whether I wanted them to or not.

"Pen, would you look at me?" he asked when we were almost home.

"No."

"Dammit, Pen, look at me."

I turned my shimmering eyes to him. "What?"

"Not getting into it in the car, but we need to talk when we get home."

"There's nothing to talk about."

"Bullshit, there's nothing to talk about. You telling me you forgot you just said you loved me?"

"Eyes on the road," I warned. "We don't want to die at an intersection."

He shot me a look like he had plenty to say, but not until we were safely inside the house—no witnesses.

We turned up our drive to find a silver Mercedes SL Roadster blocking our garage.

Gretchen.

She opened her door at the same time Ant and I did.

And my sister rushed into my husband's arms.

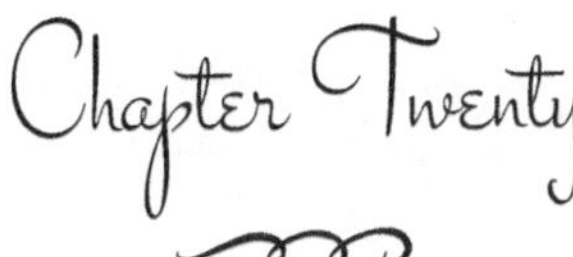

Chapter Twenty

"Come on in," I said, taking the house keys from Ant, who still had Gretch wrapped in his arms with her head buried against his chest as she sobbed. I unlocked the door, dropped my clutch on the demilune table next to the door, and said, "Let me put some coffee on," to apparently no one because neither of them was listening to me.

I slipped off my flip-flops and walked to the kitchen, where I filled the coffee carafe with water and scooped our expensive, fair-trade Columbian grounds into the filter. This gave them time to talk while I waited for the java to brew.

When I walked back out with the tray of mugs and the coffee pot, cream, and sugar, Gretchen was curled up against Ant on the sofa in the den.

"What happened?" I asked. Ant shook his head at me like I wasn't supposed to ask. I bit back my hurt to fix both of their coffees the way I knew they both liked it, then quietly excused myself from the situation, leaning against the wall to listen.

As I waited, my sister cried harder. "I have to find a job and Gabby's apartment is so small," she said. "It didn't seem that small before I moved in. But the second bedroom wouldn't hold all my clothes let alone my clothes and shoes." She sniffled loudly. "Ant, I tried to buy a Prada bag for interviews and my card was declined —*declined*. Do you know how humiliating that is?"

Probably as humiliating as getting dumped by your fiancée a month before your wedding and being forced to marry her sister instead.

"What can we do for you, Gretch?" I asked. We might not be friends but she was still my sister.

"I'm not here for you," she said. "You can go." Uh—excuse me?

"*Gretchen*," Ant admonished indulgently. "Not nice."

Not nice? That was really all he had for her? I know I messed up by telling him that I loved him, but come on.

I hesitated at the archway to see if he noticed my absence and no. "It'll be okay," he consoled my sister. "Just try to stop crying." And that was my cue. I calmly walked upstairs to our bedroom without letting that first tear fall. Then I changed out of my fancy dress to jeans and a T-shirt, packed what essentials I would need for the time being in my suitcase, along with hefting my laptop bag over my shoulder.

This was supposed to be my home. She dumped him—and I know why she did it—but I was the one who showed up in the dress and said my vows. He flew off the handle at our fathers at that dinner, but my sister tells me that I can go and nothing? It took me a bit to decide what to do here, but—and this was hard —I figured the best thing was for me to leave. I made things uncomfortable by blurting that I loved him. Maybe before Gretchen showed we might have worked it out, but with her here, just no. Having that humiliating conversation with my sister in listening distance? She'd never let me live it down.

After a few more minutes of waiting to see if my husband cared enough to come check on me, I decided I spent enough time on my fool's errand. This one broke my heart, but before I left, I took off my beautiful engagement ring that meant so much to Ant, setting it on the bedside table with a note that said: *Thank you for letting me wear this. Best, Pen.*

Then I walked back downstairs with my suitcase in tow to the garage and he never even noticed, so busy with my crying sister. Why would she even come back here? She dumped him. She dumped my husband. *Okay, don't cry, Pen. Not yet.*

"We had a good run," I whispered as I closed the door behind me.

I opened the garage door and backed out around Gretchen's convertible and headed back to my parents' home. Halfway there, I realized that I no longer had a key, so I pulled a three-point turn in the other direction and headed for the only other place I knew to go.

It was late and I felt bad for bothering her, but I didn't know what else to do. I pressed the buzzer to her apartment and waited.

"Hello?" Sierra's voice came through the speaker, groggy, as if I'd caught her sleeping, which given the time, seemed highly probable.

"Sierra?" That was as much as I got out before the waterworks started and couldn't be turned off for anything.

"Pen?" she asked, and the door unlocked, allowing me to enter. Before it closed behind me, she shot down the stairs, looking around. "Where's Ant?"

"With..." I hiccupped. "With my sister."

"Oh, *Pen*." She hugged me in the hallway, then helped me lug my bag up to her apartment. Inside, she rolled my bag to the spare room, then locked up. "Sit. Looks like you got tea to spill."

I started gushing a fresh round of tears, vaguely aware of Sierra moving around in her kitchen. She came back with a bottle of the cheapest, *get-you-drunk super-quick* tequila and two shot glasses.

She poured each of us a shot and I threw mine back the moment she stopped pouring. I started from the point in the night when things started going downhill with Ant and me when I'd stupidly said I loved him right through his admonishment because I dared ask my sister what was wrong. I finished crying to her about leaving without him even being aware that I'd gone, taking several more shots along the way. It'd be safe to say I got good and sloshed.

"I honestly can't believe he'd do that," she slurred, shaking her head.

"What's not to believe?" I hiccupped again, this time from the booze rather than the crying. "I love him. He sexes me. Basically, I'm a live-in booty call. That's all we had, friendship and sex. I waited for him to come check on me and nope." I popped the "p" at the end of nope because that was how drunk Pen be.

"But I thought—"

"Things were going so well, too," I said, cutting her off. "We even started planning a Friendsgiving for this year. In the span of an hour, I went from having everything I ever wanted to being broke and homelesh—*lesss*." I exaggerated the less. I felt the tears start up again. It went that way until about four in the morning when Sierra walked me to the spare room. I fell face-first onto the mattress. "I think I'm gonna move," I said. "I'll miss you and Gloria, but it's for the best."

That was the last thing either of us said. The light clicked off and so did my mind.

"Come on, up lazy bones."

I swatted at the soulless intruder who clearly didn't understand my hungover or heartbroken state. "Go away," I said into the pillow, trying to block out the light by pressing my face against the fabric.

"Shower. We're going away for the weekend," Sierra said and I sighed all the sighs of a put-out houseguest, but as she'd so kindly taken pity on me last night, with great effort, I pushed up, flinging myself off the bed. She had hot coffee and ibuprofen for me.

With nothing for it, I popped the pills with a hot swig of brew and dragged my sorry butt into her bathroom to shower. Like always, she was right. The shower made me feel so much better.

Today I decided on ultra-comfy-casual with a pair of distressed blue jeans and a lightweight olive green sweatshirt that hung off one shoulder. My olive green Toms, light makeup, and a messy braid completed the look. I called it stylish heartbreak.

Sierra dressed similarly but replace the sweatshirt with a sweater and adjust for colors. She had a small overnight bag packed for me resting on the bed.

"Where are we going?" I asked.

"It's a surprise. Let's go. We can grab breakfast on our way."

Before making it to the door, I searched around her sofa. "Have you seen my phone?"

"Did you leave it in your car?"

Hmm... well, that was a good question. "We can look when we get to the parking lot."

And no. I forgot my phone at Ant's place. That, or, pixies had spirited it away to the land of fae during the night. One more thing to remember when I cleared the rest of my stuff out.

She pulled her phone out and sent off a quick text.

"Who are you texting?" I asked nosily.

"Oh—*um*, just Glory."

"She coming?"

"She can't," Sierra said as she quickly shoved her phone into her pocket.

I couldn't believe it—she drove us to Cleveland to see the Rock & Roll Hall of Fame. We checked into our hotel and then drove to the museum. A nice couple from the Netherlands took a picture of Sierra and me being idiots, posing in front of the giant, red LONG LIVE ROCK sign, then we took a few for them.

Si texted back and forth with Gloria several times throughout the day. I wanted to text "hi" but she said Glory had to go.

We literally stayed until they kicked us out. There was just too much to see. A couple of favorites included the Century of Music display and David Bowie's Ziggy Stardust costumes. Then, sufficiently hungry, we headed down to a local brewery that came highly recommended to us for super juicy, drippy burgers and of course, beer.

Sierra posted everything on her social media accounts.

Without a phone, I felt a bit naked because I couldn't take pictures—but then again, I'd have to create accounts to begin with to post them. Von Duttons were too good for social media, so my parents never permitted me to have any. Only the low class felt the need to upload every moment of their lives. Then, once I'd become a McCain, there just hadn't been time. I guess one good thing to come out of that was it saved me from the embarrassment of having to update my relationship status from '*Married*' to '*It's complicated.*'

But no—I shook my head to get rid of those thoughts. My friend went through a lot of trouble to get my mind off my failed marriage. I squared my shoulders, determined to be present for this trip.

That night, she took me clubbing. Me—Penelope von Dutton-McCa—that was another thing I needed to get used to. I'd just started getting into the swing of calling myself a McCain and now it appeared I was on my way back to plain, old Von Dutton.

Two really cute men zeroed in on us almost as soon as we entered the club, wanting to buy us drinks. Now, I never went clubbing, but I knew the rules of safety. You never let a man buy you a drink lest he felt like you owed him something in return, and whether or not my husband cared if I saw other people, I wouldn't break my marriage vows. Thus, I wasn't sleeping with any dude until probably forever, but certainly until my marriage was officially dissolved. They sure were fun to dance with, though.

Thank goodness the one dancing with me, Glen, had blond hair and brown eyes. The other one, although he didn't look a lot like Ant, reminded me a bit too much of the man my heart needed to forget.

We danced until closing time with Sierra snapping off shots of us to post intermittently throughout the night.

Finally, we made it back to our hotel and when my head hit the pillow, that was all she wrote.

On Sunday morning, we found a diner at which to eat our body weights in pancakes and then proceeded to take in the other sights that Cleveland had to offer, including hitting up the baked goods and produce vendors at the West Side Market.

But alas, she had to work tomorrow and I needed to get my life together, so we decided to head back home.

After a three-hour trip back, we pulled into her complex. I half-expected Ant to somehow have found out I was with Sierra and be waiting here to bring me home with him. It was funny the things we could try to convince ourselves of.

At least with me gone, Ant had one less complication to deal with.

Why didn't I get that chance?

Chapter Twenty-One

When Sierra arrived home from work the next day, I had cleaned the entire apartment and dinner waited piping hot on the table. I stuffed and roasted a pork loin, smashed new potatoes with butter and fresh parsley, and served up baby asparagus with hollandaise—*thank you, Food Network.*

Although I desperately wanted a moscato, I just couldn't get myself to buy one, not yet. So instead, I chilled a bottle of a California Riesling.

"Are you kidding me?" she said as she set her bag down on the small table under her key hook. "Pen, this is amazing. Will you be *my* wife?"

I laughed. "I might have to be if I can't find a job." I gestured to the table. "Please, sit."

"Let me wash my hands and I'm all over this—*wow.*"

She took the opportunity to change into her lounge clothes before she joined me at the table.

Sierra filled her plate then took a large bite of the tender pork and I swear her eyes rolled back in her head. "Oh my god, you either have magic hands or a secret culinary degree to make this."

"I'm glad you like it." Knowing I could pull my weight

around here as part of my rent made me feel a hell of a lot better about asking what I needed to ask. Time to pull up my big girl panties. "Is it all right if I stay here with you until I get a job and find a place?" I sucked in a breath. "I'll do all the cooking and cleaning to offset part of my rent. If it ever gets too much, you can ask me to leave without any argument from me. I'd rather have your friendship, but I just can't go back to my parents' house. And if I can't find a job, I'll auction off all my stuff at one of those online marketplaces, then I'll move down to Central America, where the cost of living is lower."

She shot me some serious side-eye. "Do you hear yourself?"

"Uh—*yeah*. I'm the one who just went off on a five-minute spiel."

"You're not moving to Central America. I just got you back. I'm not losing you again."

My broken heart felt lighter than it had in days. "I don't deserve you."

She flipped her hand in the air. "No one does—well, except for Gloria, but that's because she's too good for any of us. But you have really good taste in friends, so brownie points for that."

"You know I love you, Sierra."

"I know. I wouldn't think nearly as highly of you if you didn't." She raised her glass to me and I raised mine to her in return before we each took a sip of wine and then burst out into a fit of giggles.

A ping notification from Sierra's text message went off. She looked down at it, then set her fork down to respond.

"Are you expecting someone tonight? I can go for a drive for a while if you want privacy. But fair warning, if he doesn't profess his undying love for you, walk away. You don't want to end up as an old spinster lady who hates everything to do with love except for her hundred cats like me."

"You aren't a spinster and you don't own even one cat."

"I'm projecting into the future."

"My guess—your husband will have a thing or two to say about that."

"*Husband?*" Why did she have to go and bring him up? I shoved my plate away from me. "I only have a husband in the most technical terms. *My guess* is that *technical* will become *nonexistent* real soon."

"You are going to be *so* embarrassed when he shows to collect you. You and all your whiny, '*waa—my husband doesn't love me*' nonsense."

"What? We literally just went over this. You said I could move in here because of it."

"I never actually said you could move in, just that you aren't moving to Central America."

I froze. Okay—*what?* "Fine. I'll be out before you get home from work tomorrow."

"I know you will."

Jeez, where'd my sweet, understanding, took-me-to-Cleavland friend go? The hostility ran deep with this doppelgänger of *my* Sierra. I closed my eyes, pinching the bridge of my nose. "Listen," I said. "It's been three days. He hasn't shown. I doubt he even knows I'm gone."

"You sure about that?"

"Yes, I'm sure about that."

"Hmm... well here I thought your husband called me Friday night worried out of his mind that you were gone."

My mouth dropped open. "Excuse me?"

"Yup. We've been texting all weekend. I told him to get Gretchen gone and that I'd watch out for you while he dealt with that."

"But he still—"

"He wanted to drive over here that night and bring you home. I told him not to. You were in no state to deal with any of that and I didn't want you two waking my neighbors. I like this apartment."

"Si, he doesn't love me."

She stood from the table walking over to the door. "Girlfriend, if you think that, then you haven't been paying attention," she replied as she pressed the button to unlock the outside door.

It took less than a minute between her pressing the button to having someone knock, no that was no ordinary knock. They pounded with extreme urgency. Sierra casually opened the door and Ant rushed inside, straight over to me, where he hauled me from my seat, pushing me up against the wall behind the table, and pressed the hardest, angriest, most—I don't know, relieved?—kiss imaginable to my very shocked lips.

"Do you know how worried I was? I go up to find you after getting Gretch calmed down and you're nowhere in the house. Some of your stuff is missing. You left me my ring for Christ's sake. What is wrong with you, woman? I called Sierra but she said you weren't there, then your parents, Rochester, Gloria, hell—I even called Gabby to see if you'd gone there. I finally got a hold of Sierra again because I needed help looking for you and I couldn't just call you—what were you thinking leaving your damn phone at the house? And she tells me you showed up and you're a quarter of a bottle down in Tequila."

"To be fair, Sierra helped with that bottle. I was drunk and it was late so I went to sleep—wait, I don't get it, why'd you call Sierra Friday night?"

"Technically, it was Saturday morning," Sierra said and I shot her the glare of all glares.

"Why didn't you tell me he called?" I asked Si accusingly.

"Because you were so sure things were over and then too drunk to listen to reason. So I came up with a plan that I thought might help you get your head on straight. Time away from the problem usually does the trick. I'm not sorry."

Okay, well, to be honest, I wasn't necessarily sorry either. She's probably right. I wouldn't have listened to him. I'd felt too hurt to listen.

"Why would you leave?" he asked.

"Well..." I sucked in a harsh breath. "Why would I stay?"

"Because you love me. You told me so earlier that night."

"Right. But you got real weird afterward and said 'we need to talk'. I know what that means. I'm not stupid. We were friends who had a lot of sex and I ruined it by dropping the L bomb. Everyone knows I was the consolation bride, the stand-in." My shoulders slumped. I hated speaking those words out loud.

"Conso—I can't—" He looked to Sierra. "I'm taking her home. We'll be back for her things tomorrow."

Ant totally flipped me over his shoulder in a fireman's hold to carry me out of Sierra's apartment. I didn't even have my purse. He didn't stop until he dropped me into the front seat of the Jag and buckled me in himself. Then he rounded the hood, a man on a mission, slid in the driver's seat, and took off for home.

We pulled into the garage. My sister's Merc was gone. As Ant swept me from the car, he flipped me over his shoulder again and marched us upstairs to the bedroom, where he dropped me onto the mattress.

I didn't know what to say. I cooked dinner at Sierra's. Ant showed up, then kidnapped me to bring me home—I should've been paying attention to him rather than going over the sequence of the evening's events because the next thing I knew, my T-shirt was up over my head.

"What are you doing?" I asked.

"What am I doing? I'm going to have the wildest makeup sex imaginable with my wife. Then I'm going to make love to her nice and slow. Then we're going to talk because it appears we both have a lot to answer for."

Wild makeup sex? Did I even want to have wild makeup sex with Ant? That was a stupid question, of course, I wanted any kind of sex I could get from the man. He knew all the right buttons to press.

And as it turned out, wild makeup sex blew wild honeymoon sex away and wild honeymoon sex had been the best sex of my life up till this point.

But nothing, and I truly meant *nothing*, compared to

Stanton McCain making love to me. He rolled in the bed to capture me underneath his strong body. The heat of him growing in intensity. "Wrap your leg around my hip, sweetheart." He growled low in my ear and I did it right away. How could I not? He wielded that sexy growl like a weapon that he aimed right at my libido.

He bent his neck in to capture any sound I might've made with his mouth in a life-reaffirming kiss that outdid any other kiss in the history of kisses. The life it reaffirmed was the life that he and I shared together. My heart hammered against my ribcage even as our bodies took things excruciatingly slow, drawing out each and every touch.

"First..." He reached over to the bedside table, wrenched open the drawer, and stuck his hand inside. He pulled something out. A something I one hundred percent approved of when he slid my engagement ring up my finger. "Unless it no longer fits you, don't you ever take this off again. Then we'll get it resized and it will go back where it belongs."

"Ant."

He was hot and hard again. I felt him at my opening. "We have a problem," he said as he slid inside, "you talk to me." He pressed his forehead to mine as he pushed all the way home. "What you don't do is leave me, Pen."

And then he began to move with long, drawn-out strokes, the torturous kind that left a woman senseless, breathless, and full of wonder.

I squeezed my eyes closed, allowing the pleasure to spread over my entire body. I loved this man. He knew I loved him.

He kissed me again on a down glide. "I love you, Pen." His breaths started coming harder, ragged. "I've been in love with you since that trip the families took to Turks and Caicos together."

"You... *have?*" My breath hitched. "That was like six years ago."

"*Mm...* but I'd been with Gretch so long... how did I tell you?" He threw a twist in and my heart might've just stopped. I might have actually been deceased at the moment. "Your loyalty to the family ... would've never... let you be with me."

"Probably not."

"But everything we did... the kayaking... the talks on the beach... how real you were... with me... I realized... it was you, Pen."

"But—*oh God!*—you proposed to Gretch."

"Yeah, I did... what was expected of me... and proposed to Gretch. But it's you... you own my heart, Pen."

I closed my eyes, letting all the sensations wash over me. Gold spots popped behind my closed eyes and then the rush of ecstasy made me feel as if I were flying.

His whole body grew taut to the point that his muscles began to spasm. Ant threw his head back. "Pen," he roared my name like a promise given to the universe that I was truly the one he loved.

Then he collapsed on top of me. My Ant. My beautiful, beautiful Ant. We took several moments to collect ourselves, but even after, we were never out of touching range. He cradled me in his arms. My head rested on his pillow along with him.

"Why'd you leave, Pen?" he finally asked the ten-million-dollar question.

"I told you I loved you in the car, but then it got awkward. Then, we pull into the driveway and there's my sister. She runs into your arms and you let her like she was still your girlfriend."

"She's my friend, Pen. She needed a shoulder."

"But when I brought out the coffee and asked what was wrong, you shushed me. If I'd really meant anything to you, then why didn't you let me help her with you? You didn't even know when I'd left."

"Shit—*sweetheart*, I'm so sorry. I guess I fell back into those old habits of giving your sister everything she wanted, which at that moment meant my attention. I never meant to hurt you. I was planning to tell you how I felt once we got inside the house. That's why I didn't say it back. What I feel for you is too big to be spoken on a car ride."

"I just—"

He moved in to kiss me again. "I was so damn relieved when Gretch took off with Gabby. I thought, now I just have to get Pen to go out with me. But then, our parents took care of that too. I was so glad to be married to you. When you said we should do it —I felt like I could break out into some asinine song, it made me that happy."

"But you didn't even kiss me."

"Because we'd been friends for so long and I'd just broken up with your sister. I had to get a feel for how you were handling things first or risk totally alienating you."

That actually made sense.

"Why'd my sister come here to you instead of me? I'm her sister."

He scoffed. "Get this—she wanted me to marry her to get the family's money back."

"She *what?*"

"Yeah, she said that we could have Gabby move in with us and that she'd share a room with Gabby and I could have all the flings I wanted as long as I kept them on the down low."

"But what about me? You both were already married."

"She figured we could both get annulments and do a quickie wedding."

"But again, what about me? Didn't she take me into consideration at all?"

"Sorry, sweetheart. She didn't. I kept things amicable, even though she pissed me off by suggesting we marry. But then I asked what did I get out of the arrangement, and she said I didn't have to live with the embarrassment of being married to her stand-in any longer."

I gasped.

"I kicked her out, Pen. No one gets to talk about my wife like that. You are *nobody's* stand-in."

If anyone ever wondered why I suffered from self-esteem issues, there you go. No, we weren't close, but come on. We were sisters for crying out loud. How could you be that callous toward your sister?

Tears pricked my eyes, both from my sister's betrayal and Ant's words of love. "I love you, Stanton McCain."

"That's good because I love you, Penelope von Dutton-McCain."

"You should probably show me how much," I teased, flinging my leg over his hip.

Chapter Twenty-Two

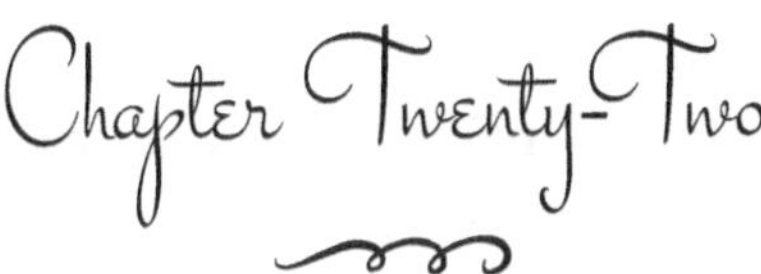

"**C**ome on in." I greeted Gloria and her plus one, a friend from work who was in the midst of her own man troubles. Murielle. A cute, sassy blonde who despite it being our first meeting, we all adored her. I knew a thing or two about her love woes: in love with a man who didn't love you back. Been there. Done that. Designed the T-shirt, myself.

We'd given the staff the night off to spend with their families at their own Thanksgiving celebrations. As it turned out, neither Ant nor I had the heart to fire most of them before the holidays.

They did come in handy, especially after the contractor finished my studio. I knew in the coming years Ant was going to regret giving me that. My studio was the other man in our relationship. Although my husband didn't seem to mind after the day we'd *eh-hemmed* on a large block of clay. He told me that when that block became a masterpiece, it had to go in our bedroom because the memories were too good to let go.

I planned to give him something special for Christmas.

Rochester and Alessandra showed.

Sierra showed without a plus one.

Cormac and Liz showed excited about a plus one to come. I mean, what wonderful news.

Ant and I even went as far as to take pity on Gretchen and Gabby and invited them to dinner too. Gabby had a large family that we figured they'd choose to dine with, but as we'd been estranged since the night Gretchen showed up here crying in Ant's arms, we'd extended the olive branch. They didn't show. I wasn't too broken up about it. I wanted to maintain my friendship with Gabby more than I actually cared about a relationship with my sister. It sounded cruel, yes. But she hurt me—soul-deep hurt me. Gretchen never even deigned an apology for trying to break up my marriage. I could hardly believe anyone would blame me for cutting ties with her altogether. *I* found it hard to believe that Gabby stayed with my sister after her visit to our home. Though, maybe Gretchen never told her. That was for them to figure out.

My darling husband grilled the turkey with mesquite wood on the outdoor grill while I prepared the sides. I may have gotten a little carried away, but this was our very first Friendsgiving. Mashed potatoes. Sweet potatoes. Mac and cheese. Green bean casserole. Corn casserole. Stuffing. Salad. Crudités. Deviled eggs. Cranberry relish. Sautéed greens. Dinner rolls, and four kinds of pies. We had enough food to feed half the city. I didn't want to let anyone down.

We offered red wines, white wines, and our cherished moscato. I didn't give two cares whether you drank red with poultry or not. At our celebration, we drank what we loved.

What we didn't expect—and truly, this would blow anyone's mind—was for Ant's mother to show. We hadn't spoken to any of the parents since that disastrous dinner.

"Mother?" Ant said, clearly as shocked as any of us. "What are you doing here?"

"I wanted to see my only son and his wife on Thanksgiving—sue me."

I bumped him with my hip, gesturing for her to enter. "Come on in, Helena."

It took him a second, but he held the door open wide for her. "Yes, come on in, Mother."

Well, that started the beginning of the end with our "Friends-giving" as Gerald showed up next to "get his wife," but he ended up staying for food. The last to arrive were Philip and Evelyn.

"I get why your mother showed," I said to Ant in a private moment in our kitchen, "but if your father or my parents say one thing—"

"They're gone," he assured me. "This is our home and I won't have anyone disrespecting us, our friends, but especially you." He tugged on my dress to bring me closer, and he wrapped his arms around my waist as he bent in to kiss me. "No one is ruining my first holiday with my wife." I'd opted for a camel-colored, long-sleeved wrap dress from the 1970s with my tall brown boots. I sort of reveled in how much it killed my mother to hold her tongue. I saw it on her face every time she looked at me. And yes, I accepted that evil side of my personality, but come on, didn't I deserve a little bit of evil after what she'd put me through—just this once?

"They couldn't possibly," I said back. "Not as long as I have you here with me."

My words came back to haunt me once those four were together again because the "it's too late for city council, but we think you could run for (*fill in the blank*)" talk started right up where they'd left off. It took everything I had not to let them get to me. *Everything*.

Part of not letting them get to me included outright ignoring them as best as possible—a practice of which Ant followed suit. We moved to the den after dinner to play games. Partly because we loved playing games and partly because we hoped it would get those four to leave.

Thankfully, the universe listened to our prayers.

The rest of the evening went exactly how a celebration should go. That was to say, swimmingly.

After everyone had left and we'd gotten the food put away, Ant and I walked upstairs to our room to get ready for bed.

"Let's take a bath," he said and I loved that idea. He got the wine while I got the water going. Then we both stripped down and he sat in the water first, giving me a backrest to lean against with his chest.

I took a sip of my wine. "What are we going to do about them?" I asked. He knew exactly to whom I referred. How could he not?

"I don't know. I meant what I said. We're taking time to just be us for a while."

"Well, you know I completely support that decision, my love."

He nipped my cheek then took a drink of his wine.

"I'm in support of most of the decisions you make," I said, laughing from the way his breath tickled my skin.

"Oh, yeah? Then I've decided we're moving to Portugal."

"Why Portugal?"

"Because it's not anywhere they'd expect us to go and if they can't find us, then they can't hound us."

"I can get behind that," I agreed.

He nipped at my neck this time. "Not before I get behind you."

And boy, did he mean it.

So *not* the consolation...

* * *

Thank you for reading! If you loved meeting Stanton and Penelope, then you really want to join my SASSY CHICK ARMY NEWSLETTER where you get a bonus story to celebrate Pen and Ant's fifth wedding anniversary. Trust me, you don't want to miss it!

Keep scrolling to read the first chapter of MARRIAGE (RED, WHITE &) BLUES. Book two in the Unexpectedly Married Series.

If you haven't read my first Rom-Com series yet, let me introduce you to SKYDIVING, SKINNY-DIPPING & OTHER WAYS to ENJOY YOUR FAKE BOYFRIEND, you can read it below.

CLICK HERE TO READ SKYDIVING... >>

Do you love sweet fur-babies? Read the HOLIDAY BITES SERIES starting with ALWAYS MINE

I appreciate your help in spreading the word, including telling a friend not only about my rom-coms, but about my romantic suspense, too. The Brimstone Lords. The Bedlam Horde. Reviews help readers find books! Please leave a review on your favorite book site. A review on Amazon helps the most.

Now, how about reading the first chapter from **Marriage (Red, White &) Blues**

Chapter One

"Bye," I called out to Pen and Ant, who stood in their doorway waving goodbye to me. They had that ridiculously gorgeous, ridiculously cute couple thing going on. Given the breeze tonight, Pen's chestnut ponytail kept whipping him in the face, while his dark hair had just enough length to ripple like water. I laughed, taking them in because Ant kept swiping her hair from his mouth as they stood out on their stoop waiting for me to reach my car. Our other best friend Sierra already made it to hers. Although Ant and Pen lived in a highbrow neighborhood in Grosse Pointe Shores, they always stood out on their stoop until Sierra and I made it to our cars and locked the doors. I never understood why. They lived in one of the safest neighborhoods in Michigan. In this case, money equaled security. And let me just say, they had a lot of... *security*. Please don't take me wrong, no sour grapes on my part. I loved my friends and wished them nothing but the best. Just—sometimes it hit me how different the lives were that we led and I felt like by this point in my life, I should've somehow been further ahead than I was now. For instance:

Ant drove a Jag.

Pen drove a Merc.

Sierra drove an Audi.

I drove a Subaru Outback. Yes, a Subaru happened to be a perfectly acceptable car. One of the first times I'd driven in this neighborhood, a neighbor stopped me to find out my reason for being there. Pen and Ant were furious when they'd found out but furious or not, it didn't change the fact that one of us didn't belong here—guess which one? They never tried to make me feel inferior. My friends were all great people. It just came along with always being the poor friend. The girl who usually tried to back out of events due to lack of funds, but ended up going because friends paid my way. They insisted, I *swear*.

A little backstory: We'd met at a private school I'd thankfully been smart enough to get scholarships to attend. Then Pen and Ant had gone to Brown after high school. Sierra had flown off to Princeton. I'd gone the U of M route. A great school that again, I'd earned a full ride to attend. Unfortunately, even with a U of M degree under my belt, I didn't earn enough to buy a Jag, a Merc, or an Audi.

My job was okay. I worked in HR for the Social Security Administration. That meant I didn't have to deal with angry customers, only angry employees. I drove the thirty minutes back home, where I lived with my mother in a modest home in Beverly Hills—the Michigan town, *not* the star-studded California odyssey.

When the garage door opened, I found the garage empty. Mom should've been home this time of night. Since Dad passed from cancer right after I'd graduated high school, she rarely left the house for anything other than work or grocery shopping, despite how often I tried to get her to go out with her old friends. That was the whole reason I'd stayed in Michigan and gone to U of M instead of attending the myriad of other prestigious schools that wanted me out of state. I'd received full-ride offers all over the country. But Mom needed me close. Could she have finally taken my advice or did I need to panic?

After parking and closing the garage door, I walked into the house through the utility room.

"Mom?" I shouted, just in case she'd taken her car to the shop or something. Hmm... no answer.

I pulled my phone from my purse to call her because what if she needed me? But before I pressed her contact button, I found an unread text from her from earlier this evening.

Mom: *Gloria, I finally took your advice and am out with a friend from work tonight. Have fun with Sierra and Penelope.*

Wait—*what*? Talk about being gobsmacked. My mom had actually taken my advice and gone out with a friend from work again. I hoped this meant she finally started healing.

After watching Netflix for a little while, I decided to go to bed. Tomorrow, being Saturday, meant a busy day volunteering down at the animal shelter. To be nice, I left one light on for my mom so she didn't walk into complete darkness when she came home.

The next morning, I showered and dressed, then went down to the kitchen to grab a bite to eat before heading to the shelter. Mom forgot to turn the kitchen light off. Mom *forgot* to turn the *light off*? She never forgot. She must've had a good time last night for that to happen. I switched it off for her, then went to the garage... which still only housed *my* car.

Maybe she'd had too much to drink and a friend drove her home? But surely if my mom had been drunk last night, she'd have woken me up from all the noise she made trying to be quiet on her way up to her room. The woman rarely drank more than a glass of wine on a holiday thus, she could *not* handle her liquor. So if not too drunk to drive home, then where in the hell was my mother?

Cue the panic. *Five... Four... Three... Two...* And *now*. I raced back inside the house up to my mom's room, throwing open the door to be met by an empty bed. One that clearly hadn't been slept in.

No, no, no... Scenes from horror movies started playing out in my head. Irrational? Possibly—but this was my one remaining parent. I couldn't lose her too. I checked my phone for eerie voice-mails or ransom calls—yes, I realized no one would kidnap *my* mother for ransom but remember, panic. Sure enough, I found another text from her.

Mom: *Gloria, sweetheart. I won't be home tonight. Carl asked me to go home with him... and I agreed. I'm so nervous. Love you, sweetheart.*

Carl? My mom's "friend from work" was named Carl, and he'd asked her home and she'd felt comfortable enough to say *yes*? Just how long had *Carl* been a friend?

Still feeling upset by the whole situation, I hopped in my Outback to head to the only place that I knew would make me feel better.

As always, it worked, taking my mind off my troubles for several blissful hours.

After spending the day taking care of all things furry—young and old—I went home, walking in to find out my mother and Carl had apparently been close friends for a while. I mean, if the way they were making out like teenagers on the sofa meant anything.

"Gloria?" My mom startled. Uh, I lived here, so I couldn't see getting so surprised. A tall, broad-shouldered African-American man pushed up off my mom, and when he turned around— whoa! Carl was hot, to boot. *Go, Mom!*

"Gloria," Carl said, approaching me with his hand out. "It's good to finally meet you. I've been trying to get your mom to introduce us for the last year."

I'm sorry, did he say *the last year*?

"You two... have been friends for the *last year*?" My voice might have risen at the end there, but I had the presence of mind to shake his hand. Carl looked concerned. Mom just looked guilty. "Look, Mom, you're an adult. You don't have to report to me, but it would've been nice to know you'd met someone. This is huge and you didn't think to tell me?"

The three of us stood there in this sort of standstill and as I took her in, I realized that I didn't know her anymore. We didn't look alike. With her trimmer figure, cute brown bob, and hazel eyes, when people who didn't know us saw us together, they thought we were friends. Now, I didn't even feel like a friend.

"I just wanted—"

I held my hand up. Hurt didn't begin to cover how I felt about this situation. "It's very nice to meet you, Carl. I hope you'll come around more often now. I'm heading up to my room." Then over my shoulder, I threw out a, "Carry on."

It wasn't my proudest moment. I ran up the stairs with tears in my eyes like a damn teenager. Talk about the drama! But it couldn't be helped. When I reached my room, I called Sierra—or I tried to call Sierra. She didn't answer. That was weird. I looked at the time. She shouldn't have been sleeping unless she had a headache or something. I called again, worried about her now.

This time, she answered. "Gloria, hey, sweetie. This isn't a good time."

"Oh, okay. Are you on a date?"

"No. I'm at the movies with Beth from work. We're watching that new comedy *She Shed*." *She Shed*? My stomach sank, sank right to the damn floor. Sierra and I were supposed to go see that together. "I'll let you know how it is."

"Yeah, okay... sure. Have fun." I disconnected the call determined not to cry and then immediately pressed Pen's contact.

She answered on the first ring. "Hey, Gloria..." She giggled.

"Hey, Gloria," Ant said in the background. "Pen's going to have to call you back. She's about ready to be very distracted."

"*Ant*," Pen admonished him.

"It's okay. Don't behave," I said, laughing, although I really didn't feel it.

"Don't plan on it," he said right before I hung up.

Good. Great. Okay. So my mother lied to me for a year, Sierra broke plans with me to hang out with a different friend and Pen was too wrapped up in marital bliss to bother with me. So what? I was an independent woman. The time had come for me to start acting like it.

While I sat in my room alone, I opened my laptop and pulled up a blank Word doc. At the top, I typed: *Change Gloria's Life.* For the next hour I planned on how to make that happen. Mom had a new man. Maybe I needed a man. Sierra had new friends. Maybe I needed new friends, too. Pen and Ant had loads of sex. No maybe about this one. I couldn't remember the last time I'd sweated in the sheets from more than the flu.

Everything sort of went by in a blur from that night on.

I checked my bank account to see about my savings. Then I applied for a passport and got that expedited to me. Even expedited, it took a while to arrive, which gave me more time to save up money. Finally, I quit my job. Yeah, I quit my job. Why? Because *backpacking* across *Europe*! Yes, me. It was number four on the *Change Gloria's Life* document—you know, behind a new man, new friends, and loads of sex.

Nothing was keeping me here. Mom spent most nights with Carl now that they'd broken the seal on that one. We went from talking every day to radio silence unless *I* texted *her.* I saw my friends occasionally. And by friends, I meant Pen and Ant. I wasn't ready to forgive Sierra. I didn't care that she went to a movie with a different friend. But we'd already planned to see that together and she disregarded me and my feelings. And then to say *'she'd tell me how it was'* as if I'd go see it alone? My friends had lives to live—I got that. But now I did too. I didn't tell even one of them that I was going. Why would I? None of them bothered to keep me in their life loops. Gone were the days of reliable Gloria, always around when or *if* they decided to call.

Once I landed in France, if one of them called, then I'd tell them. "Sorry, I can't go to your BBQ. I'm in France." Petty? Probably. But I was tired of being ignored. The afterthought.

Finally, the night of my big trip arrived. I flew coach. Part of me wanted that first-class experience like Pen had on her honeymoon, but my bank account outright laughed at me, stating that was a truly bad idea if I planned to stay as long as I hoped to.

After hours of being stuck between a loud snorer and a manspreader, of continually being kicked in the back of my seat, of listening to a colicky baby cry, we landed in Paris. *Paris*. As in Paris, France.

Despite being dog-ass tired and looking a mess, I smiled all the way to customs. As I planned to backpack, I'd only brought a carry-on with me—the bag all the traveler blogs said you just '*had to have'* when embarking on this kind of adventure.

Outside the airport, I flagged down a taxi. Thankfully, I'd taken four years of French in high school and minored in it in college.

The sun shone brightly, welcoming me to this first stop on my adventure. My phone rang. Sierra. Did I even want to talk to her? "Hello?" I answered because I decided yes. I wanted her to know I currently stood in *Paris* freaking *France*.

"Gloria, girl... where are you? Your mom said she went to the house and you were gone. Your note said something about a new life? What in the hell is going on?"

"Exactly like my note said. My mom spends every night with Carl. You and Pen are busy living your lives. So I decided to start living mine."

"What does that mean?"

"It means I'm in Paris."

"*Paris*. Kentucky?"

"Nope."

"Texas?"

"Wrong again."

"You don't mean France," she said. Oh, I sure as heck did.

"That's exactly where I am. I'm headed for my hostel right now."

"*Gloria...*" she sounded sad. "When will you be home?"

"Don't know. I quit my job. I'm single. I'm free, and I have a whole continent to navigate."

"Are you with anyone? That's not safe."

"Please, I fade into the background. No one knew I was making plans. No one knew I left. Nothing will happen to me."

"Gloria—"

"Listen, we just pulled up in front of the hostel. I have to go. But I'll try to call when I get the chance."

"Okay," she said. "Be careful."

Be careful? *No*—not this time. Not that I planned to take ridiculous chances, but I wanted this one time in my life to forget about being the responsible one. To chuck responsibility out the window and live life for *me*. I paid the taxi driver and went inside. White plaster walls, and thick, exposed beams on the ceiling greeted visitors. Some beautiful dried lavender in vases on small wooden tables scattered about the space. The place looked clean and the woman at the check-in smiled. Although simple, I loved everything about this hostel.

I'd reserved a private room because I wasn't quite adventurous enough to stay in the dorm rooms. Even so, a one-person room cost me about $45 a night.

After checking in, I crashed on my bed. I'd heard about jet lag but never experienced it before. Flying from Detroit to Paris made me feel a hundred years old. The rest turned out to be exactly what the doctor would've ordered. Post my nice long nap, I showered, then dressed for the day in a cute, fitted pair of cropped jeans with folded cuffs; a pretty, sagey-green, flowy, blouse; and a pair of comfortable walking sandals. A little fresh makeup and my hair in a messy braid later, I slung my crossbody bag with my money and passport over my shoulders and headed out to see what kind of trouble I could find.

As soon as I hit the pavement outside, my tummy started to grumble. Food. I needed food. Stat.

Although I'd intended to try out one of their cafés, I walked passed an outdoor market and was drawn in by the smell of fresh bread. I bought a crusty baguette, then I passed a cheese vendor and left with a beautiful, creamy brie and a Bleu de Saint-Jean, a kind of hard blue cheese. Well, if I bought the bread and cheese, then I had to get meat. I settled on a Jambon de Bayonne, which happened to be a very thinly sliced ham, much like prosciutto. The next thing I knew, I had a netted grocery bag with olives, grapes, pears, and a bottle of Pinot Grigio. The vendor even had these cute, little plastic wine glasses and a keychain corkscrew. The wine vendor's little boy saw my bag of goodies and talked me into buying a few of his homemade poppers "to scare off the birds."

Could the birds be that bad? Well, if they were, then I was prepared. If not, I helped a child earn some cash. I could live with that.

The boy must've known what I planned to do. I mean, what did one do with such a bounty? Why, picnic, of course! I wandered through the city until I found a park where I could sit and eat my lunch while looking at the beautiful Seine. Oh, and I made sure to snap plenty of pictures to document my first day.

Before tearing into my food, I uncorked the wine first to let it breathe while the sun shone down on my face, warming me. I still couldn't believe I was here.

A person passed behind me and dropped down about ten feet away. A man—no, that wasn't nearly the right descriptor because he somehow seemed elevated from that of a regular man. He over-whelmed my senses. A demigod? Possibly. All I knew was he smelled amazing. This delicate yet manly aroma wafted in the air and hung there for me to enjoy well after he'd passed by. And let me just say, his aesthetic matched his smell. And yes, I kept glancing over at the *ridiculously* handsome man. His short, dark-brown hair looked *almost* black and had these cute spiky-feathery pieces blowing around in the soft breeze. Broad shoulders but an otherwise slim physique, like a swimmer's body. He wore a pair of aviator sunglasses that gave him an air of cool as he laid out his picnic spread.

And when he did, it made me so glad that I hadn't spread my own food out yet. A gull swooped down and flew off with his loaf of bread before he could shoo it away. Then other birds decided to shoot their shots. Biting my lip, I threw one of the poppers and it cracked in the air, scaring off the birds. I jumped, not expecting it to be that loud. The poor man looked so defeated that I couldn't stop myself from laughing if I tried. I wasn't being mean. It was just... I felt his pain. I'd had those days. He needed a friend right about now, so I stood and brushed off my bottom before picking up my bag and my wine and walking over to him.

"I have a loaf of bread I can share," I said in perfect French, holding the bag up for him to see so he didn't think I was some sort of weirdo while still biting back that laugh.

"Je ne parle pas bien français?" he said as a question and it was the cutest thing. He didn't speak French well. Okay.

"English?" I asked.

He let out a slow breath. "*Yes.* I need you to know I'm actually an intelligent man. It's just... I studied Japanese in school."

He *needed* me to know? Interesting. I repeated myself, this time in English. "I have a loaf of bread I can share."

His shoulders slumped slightly. "You don't have to do that."

"I know," I replied, laughing. "But I feel bad that you lost your lunch."

"I see you feel very badly for me. Laughing always shows sympathy."

Well, that just made me laugh harder. The *watering eyes and little snort* kind of laugh.

"Tell you what," he said. "I'll take you up on your offer if you join me."

I thought about it for a second. And why not? We had a beautiful view by the the river. Didn't I come here for this? An adventure. A beautiful man wanted to eat lunch with me. Who was I to argue with that? I dropped down on the blanket he'd laid out.

"Are you American?" I asked. "You sound very American."

"Yeah. I'm from the great state of Vermont."

"Oh, I'm from Michigan."

"I could tell by your accent."

"*Excuse me.*" I was totally taken aback. "Michiganders *don't have* accents. Everyone else does." This time *he* laughed at *me*.

"I assure you, you do."

"Well, we'll just have to agree to disagree on that," I responded, though I did so smirking.

"So what's your name?" he asked.

"Gloria."

"Glory, I like it."

"Um... actually, it's Glor*ia*." No one but my dad ever called me "Glory" and he'd died going on five years ago, which meant no one *ever* called me "Glory."

"Are you sure? From what I see, Glory just seems to fit you." He pulled off his aviator glasses, narrowing his eyes as if assessing me. "What's your last name, Gloria?"

Uh... he thought Glory fit me? Why did I like that so much? It should've bothered me to hear that nickname again, but I realized I wanted nothing more than to hear *this man* call me Glory.

"You can call me Glory," I offered. Then, because my gut told me that this was a good guy and that he wasn't out to hurt me, I answered his question. "Kowalski. I'm part Irish"—I pointed to my red hair—"and part Polish."

"Gloria's Latin, did you know?"

"Yes. That's after my grandmother. But my middle name, Brianne, is Irish."

"Glory B!" he shouted and I bit my lip, shaking my head. "The woman I'm ready to eat lunch with."

"No one has teased me with that in years."

"It seemed apropos for the situation. Don't you think?"

"No." I smiled. I couldn't help it. "You're going to run that joke into the ground now, aren't you?"

"Into the ground," he agreed, nodding several times.

I rolled my eyes. "Right. So what's your name, then?"

"Blake Parker."

"Blake Parker? How very boyband of you."

"Well, I'm told my mother liked her boy bands back in the day. I'll make sure to tell her you said that next time I see her."

His eyes twinkled and he showed off a dimple at the side of his mouth every time he smiled. I made it my goal to make him smile as much as humanly possible before we parted ways.

"I see you have a wine glass. Would you like to share a bottle?" I pointed to my Pinot Grigio. "I already popped the cork."

"Thank you. I'd love to share a bottle. This couldn't have turned out better for me."

"Why's that?" I asked while pouring him some.

"Because I saw a beautiful woman sitting by the river all alone and I knew I had to meet her. Why do you think I dropped down so close?"

"That's a little creepy."

"I like to think of it as sweet. Seriously, your red hair caught my eye and then you turned your face in my direction and I sort of couldn't breathe for a moment. That's never happened to me before."

His response took me so off guard that I didn't know what to think. I was fairly certain I'd never taken a man's breath away before. Of course, I couldn't let him know that. As I struggled to figure out what to say, my mouth began speaking—worse, *flirting*—without my permission. But I *never* flirted. I didn't even know how. Still, the words kind of sounded flirty.

"Aw... flattery will get you everywhere," I said as I poured myself a glass of wine, and then popped a grape into my mouth.

"So tell me, what brings a beautiful red-headed Michigander to Paris?" He sipped his drink.

"Probably the same thing that brought an utterly handsome Vermonter. It's Paris. Does one need a specific reason?"

"For clarity, am I the handsome Vermonter in this scenario?"

"*Utterly* handsome," I reminded him, chuckling uncomfortably as I scanned the area to avoid eye contact, but then turned back to him. Blake smiled at me. That meant he like it right? In for a penny. In for a pound. Sucking up my courage, I went ahead and said what I wanted to say. "Well, since we're the only ones here, it's a safe assumption." Who was this brave, new Gloria? I liked her. I needed to get to know her better.

I watched, practically mesmerized as he tore off a hunk of baguette, smeared it with some brie, folded a piece of ham on top, and bit down. He chewed with purpose and that purpose seemed clearly to get me hot and bothered. If it wouldn't have called attention to my flushed face, I'd have fanned myself.

"So... tell me about yourself," he said.

I shrugged. "You first."

He smiled and that was all she wrote. We talked and ate until the sun looked lower in the sky and a chill drifted over the air.

"How long have we been here?" I asked, looking down at my phone.

It turned out we'd spent the last four hours talking about everything. Four hours?!

"I suppose we should get going now," Blake said and my heart sank. Even after four hours, I still felt like our time together wasn't finished.

He helped me clean up the trash and then stood. Blake held his hand out to me to help me up.

"Are you up for doing anything else together?" he asked.

Yes.

Yes.

All the yes.

I welcomed my next adventure.

Read the rest here: MARRIAGE (RED, WHITE &) BLUES

The Bedlam Horde MC

Devil's Advocate: Vlad (Book 1)

Devil's Due: Sarge (Book 2)

Devil's Work: Dark (Book 3)

Devil Incarnate: Reaper (Book 4)

Devil to Pay: Cutter (Book 5)

Devil Inside: Green (Book 6)

Brimstone Lords MC

Bossman: Undone (Brimstone Lords MC 1)

Duke: Redeemed (Brimstone Lords MC 2)

Chaos: Calmed (Brimstone Lords MC 3)

Scotch: Unraveled (Brimstone Lords MC 4)

Hero: Claimed (Brimstone Lords MC 5)

Blood: Revealed (Brimstone Lords MC 6)

Adventures in Love Series

Skydiving, Skinny-Dipping & Other Ways to Enjoy Your Fake Boyfriend

D.I.E.T. (Dating in Extreme Times)

WTF Are You Thinking?

Holiday Bites (A Lake Shores, MI World)

Baby, It's Cold Outside (Book One)

Always Be My Baby (Book Two)

Standalones

Summer of the Boy

<u>*Audio*</u>

Summer of the Boy

Skydiving, Skinny-Dipping & Other Ways to Enjoy Your Fake Boyfriend

Acknowledgments

I thank them in every book and I will continue to do so throughout the rest of my writing career. My two sons are the reason I work as hard as I do. Every mom should be lucky enough to call their children their best friends like I do.

This next one is hard. I lost my dad last year. Right in the middle of writing my last book, actually. I wasn't sure if I'd ever find my words again. My dad supported my dream to be a published author. He babysat my kids when I went to college to get my degree in writing. And although he often asked me, "When are you going to write something that people read?" I knew what he meant. When was I going to write something he'd read? Because if my dad didn't read romance, clearly no one did.

But here's the thing, he was the first one to tell anybody he talked to from a person standing in line next to him to the checkout clerk that his daughter was a published author.

Thank you, Papa, for believing in me.

About the Author

Sarah Zolton Arthur is a USA TODAY Bestselling author of pretty much all things romance, but when she's not writing sassy women in rom-coms, she loves to get down and dirty with her MC bad boys. She spends her days embracing the weirdly wonderful parts of life with her two kooky sons while pretending to be a responsible adult.

She resides in Michigan, where the winters bring cold, and the summers bring construction. The roads might have potholes, but the beaches are amazing.

Above all else, she lives by these rules. Call them Sarah's life edicts: In Sarah's world, all books have kissing and end in some form of HEA. Because even outlaw bikers need love.

www.ingramcontent.com/pod-product-compliance
Lightning Source LLC
Chambersburg PA
CBHW061533310726

48972CB00008B/2445